ESCAPE

The Arvidan Chronicles • Book One

By

Susan Trott

Copyright

Table of Contents

Chapter 1
The Day Zydee Broke

The world was dying.

For more than fifteen hundred solar cycles, the tectonics of Zydee were ripping the land apart, causing devastation to everything. The skies had grown poisonous, the scant plant life was struggling and the remaining animals were sick and dying. A few hung on, had adapted, but they were disappearing. The people called it the Age of Extinction.

Captain Thiopeta Tuatu, a decorated solar pilot from this Age, was standing by the window of her office staring out at the angry land. It was scarred with fire and steam as the volcanic eruptions continued unabated. Gliese, the star that their planet orbited, was being torn apart too.

As the planet groaned, she felt the pain. As the land was ripped apart, she felt as if her own body was being torn asunder. Tears ran down her face, quietly, her forehead rested against the glass and her breath formed clouds of steam on it. She placed her palm on the glass and pushed against the window to push back the pain, to no avail.

"We could have prevented this," she whispered. "WE COULD HAVE PREVENTED THIS!!!" she screamed at the scene beyond the glass, anger choking her words as she spoke them. She pounded her fist on the window. "We should have prevented this! Such a needless waste." Her chest heaved as she slumped on the floor, face and hand pressed against the glass.

The people of Zydee were being forced to leave their home. The scientists had done everything they could think of to save the planet and failed. Now everyone had to leave.

Zydee and her sister planets were being pulled into a newly formed binary star. Two planets had already succumbed. Astronomers had watched it happen on their high-powered telescopes. They knew what was happening, but they insisted that it would never directly affect Zydee. So many lies.

Even when the planet's crust started pulling itself apart, turning verdant valleys into burning pits of fire and lava, they said it would not destroy Zydee. When the tides became chaotic, uneven, and unpredictable and then the magnetism went wild, it started hurting other species. Migrating animals, birds, and whales got lost, and the whole species disappeared.

The most devastating event to conclude was the drying up of the seas. Zydee never had huge seas in the first place. But they evaporated when the surface started heating up. Fresh water was only deep underground now. Major lakes hung on if they were shadowed by mountains, but not enough.

Tuatu's thoughts were interrupted by the protestors screaming in the square nearby. Thousands of people were chanting, waving signs, and bellowing, hoping to be saved from the calamity enfolding around them. Still others were protesting the programs taking the people off-world, believing instead it was their fate to die with the planet. Tuatu didn't know who was more right, but either way, she was leaving. She had been given another commission, this time to Captain an ark ship.

Little did the protestors know that the Councils had already taken action. Before the Age of Extinction, before the planet had started ripping itself apart, when there was time and peace; they had a space program.

They had wanted to explore the stars and they did. Several scout ships, small by current standards, but the forerunners to new technology, were sent out across the universe. They went in search of intelligent life.

They never got any answers, and so the space program was shuttered, the technology shelved and marked secret. No one knew of this past, except for those in the military now.

Zydee was home, but it could not be for much longer. Scientific estimates had given the planet only another 20 Silences before it succumbed to the binary star. A Silence was how long it took Zydee to orbit Gliese. It had been doing this for trillions of Silences. Having so little time left was really unimaginable.

Already about thirty percent of the population on just one land mass had been lost due to the natural disasters.

Tuatu picked herself up from the floor with a heavy sigh. She opened her desk drawer and took out a small box, lovingly wrapped in silk. It contained a single seed from the tree her parents had planted when she was born. That seed had lived as long as Tuatu, but tree had perished three Cycles ago. Tuatu managed to save a single seed from the tree. It felt like her last hope; to plant the seed on a new world and have it survive. Tuatu resealed the seed into the box to preserve it.

"Perhaps I can take this box with me; plant it on the world we find and make it our new home," she mused.

She glanced at the painting hanging on her office wall that was painted by her mother, at their home before the Age of Extinction. The tree was called the Sacred Flower. It grew high in the mountains in shallow valleys. It was a tree that had foliage all the time, and grew to heights of four Avens tall. It had small leaves with clusters of brilliant pink, narrow tubular flowers that bloom once a year.

Their world had once been such a beautiful place; tall trees, fragrant with large flowers, blocked out the sun in thick forests. There had been so many flowers, the forests gave off a scent strong enough to travel the wind currents. The planet once had lots of water too, rushing rivers tumbling down rocky terrain to splash into crystal clear lakes that reflected the clouds and skies. But that was thousands of Silences ago.

Now when the comet P'shat passed on its regular schedule, its tail no longer got reflected in the rivers and lakes. It passed by without a hint of recognition. The colors of deep magenta and aubergine to lavender to violet no longer laced across the sky in delicate swirls and patterns to be reflected in the perfectly still water.

It was all that was left of them, my family, and it would be all that remained of my home. Thought Tuatu. It is precious to me. "This one seed will help me settle down on a new world if we get there," she said out loud. "Hopefully, it flourishes, and then we will too."

Straightening her shoulders and stiffening her back, Tuatu gathered the briefing notes that had been delivered that morning, and sat down to read them. They turned out to be her orders. She was given the ark ship Arvidan to command with a crew of 1,000 and 10,000 souls to protect; so named for the planet it was destined for.

The ship was one of the fully functioning ark ships designed to carry the people safely away from home, and to sustain them for as long as needed to get to a new planet. Zydeans used bond-energy to create the energy to drive the ship and its systems. It was the nature of the bond to come in bursts. It was not a switch that was turned on and left on like electricity.

The bond-energy was generated by the people who bonded. An excerpt from the Ancient Codex of Blood and Becoming:

Once upon a time we were animals of a higher order. We were not born of peace.

We came from shadow and claw, from fangs that shimmered in moonlight. Our ancestors hunted the low-born subspecies for survival, for dominance, for the thrill of the chase.

We were swift bipedal predators with the vision of hawks, the scenting of wolves, and the silence of ghosts. We ran faster than any prey, and We wore the wind like a second skin.

In those early nights, we did not love. We mated, we swarmed, we bled. But sometimes just sometimes two would bond. Not by lust, but by alignment. When a pair bonded, the very air bent to them. We could speak across oceans, build without tools, summon light from within.

Summon and control energy with a thought. Our union forged the first spark of our greater science the energy of the bond.

Bonding gave the Zydeans access to a natural power that they could bend to their will, to create, to build, to grow, to fight. It wasn't limitless, exhausting those who used it. This is why, in any endeavour, Bonded Zydeans were especially chosen for the task they excelled at. On board the ark ship, there were Bonded Zydeans who drove each ship, serving in shifts. They were never allowed to completely drain themselves, as that would be life-threatening.

The ark ships were the latest technology the Zydeans had designed. Everything on board was recycled; from capturing all moisture to purifying it, and then returning it back into liquid water, to reusing minerals and organic matter to build and grow things. With a specialized crew of 1,000, they were capable of combining energies to run the ship's systems. The colonists who traveled would spend most of their time in stasis, only being awakened upon arrival.

It was up to the Captain and her 1,000 crew to keep the ship alive so it would keep them all alive.

The decision had been made Cycles ago to ship everyone possible off world; to seek a new home. It was controversial. Protestors ran amok in every city trying to prevent the ark ships from leaving.

Tuatu felt the blaring of the siren outside as it pounded waves of sound against the building. That was the warning for another earthquake, and the ground started shaking almost immediately. More tectonic pressure released without an eruption was good news.

That was Tuatu's cue to get down to the ark. Rushing to get her go-bag, slipping her small box carefully in the center of all the clothes for protection, she threw her bag over her shoulder and ran out the door letting it slam shut behind her. It was a race down the stairs to the street as the building swayed to the rhythms of the earthquake, but she knew it would hold.

The streets were jammed with people, and finding a transport was difficult. She eventually jumped on one and pushed her way inside; and was jostled up against bodies due to standing room only. It would take her to the ark ship and that was all she needed. The transport dodged and darted between the buildings and other transports as it ascended to the ark ship.

The ark ships hovered off the ground about ten stories, so ground quakes wouldn't damage them. However, that didn't prevent a building collapse from hitting them, so the ship routinely moved around looking for holes in the city scape.

As the transport approached the ship, a doorway opened, it slipped inside and landed on a platform that was already busy with people darting this way and that. It looked like utter confusion. Tuatu was disembarking when a young man, waving his arm frantically, flagged her down.

She walked over to him, and he snapped to attention. She glanced at his insignia, Ensign.

"Permission to come aboard, Ensign Stictu?" Tuatu asked formally.

"Permission granted, sir!" he responded. "Captain, would you like me to show you to your quarters?"

"Thank you, Ensign. I know the way. Is the AI installed yet?"

"Yes, Captain, that was completed a few days ago. It's up and functional."

"Very good. That will be all Ensign."

As she worked her way through the halls of the ship she said out loud, "AI, do you hear me?"

"I do, Captain. Welcome aboard." The voice was soft pleasant, female in tone, but still synthetic. "Awaiting your first instruction."

"AI please show me to the command deck."

"Certainly." And a set of blue lights lit up on the wall in a line stretching ahead of her as she walked. They winked out as she passed. "Please follow the blue lights, Captain."

Within a few Shards, the AI had brought her to the command deck. She stood at the door and took in the machines, consoles, and equipment array across the floor. "AI, do you have a preferred method of being addressed?" She asked.

"You can call me VIRA, Captain."

"That'll be nicer, thank you VIRA."

The crew was antsy, chomping at the bit, and Tuatu sympathized. Everyone was stationed and ready to go. Lifting off was a big deal, and required all flight crew on deck to generate the startup power to escape the atmosphere.

Collectively, everyone was watching the forward screen; witnessing the scene of incredible chaos on the streets below. The last-Shard colonists were supposed to be assembled and brought to the ship, but there had been some sort of snag creating more delays. The Arvidan wasn't the only ship leaving that day, but from the panic in the people, you'd think it was the last.

The scientists had told us that this area was under an "extreme" warning. This meant that they were expecting an eruption at any Shard; an eruption that could cost the ship. That had already happened a number of times at other shipbuilding platforms. One ark ship had been loading on the ground when an earthquake had opened up a crevasse and pretty much swallowed the ship whole. An entire crew had been lost, not to mention half of their colonists.

That was the reason this ark ship was off the ground. Some fancy magnetics were being used to hover the ship. As the sirens blared the Captain started a routine of pacing across the command deck, stopping to watch the chaos and muttering to herself.

"Captain, is there a problem?" asked the AI.

"I don't understand the science that keeps the ship hovering in place," said Tuatu. "It is not my specialty. However, if an eruption had enough force, could it still damage our ship?"

"Captain, pacing won't make them move faster," said VIRA. "Yes, we could sustain damage if something exploded on the ground, or a building collapsed on top of us."

"Then why don't we move?," I snapped back and immediately regretted it. "Sorry, is there any data about that eruption?"

"No, nothing immediate. However, there is only one more shuttle to arrive and we can get out of here."

"That's good news!" Tuatu said, letting out some stress. "VIRA, make sure everyone is where they are supposed to be and that all hands are in place for the lift off. I'll be in my quarters."

"Yes, Captain."

Looking around the command deck, reminded her of just what a leap this ship represented in Zydean technology. There had been space travelers for many Silences now, but this was a generational ship. It was meant to sustain the people on it for as long as they needed. So everything was reused, from air to food to water. Even the structure of the craft was organic, a living ship with a skin made of a new element to protect everyone from space radiation while keeping in the heat.

The propulsion system was new too. It was called a "Pulse Drift" and was a Semi-FTL Burst Drive. It could sustain faster-than-light speeds for short periods of time, in energy bursts, but dropped down to sub-light between. Again, the Zydeans used Bonded minds to generate bursts of power, which is why it has the name "Bondwave energy". The command deck crew was specifically selected for this task. They had the ability to bond with the ship.

The ship knew where it was going, because navigation was done by the onboard AI. Other crew members were there to maintain the ship. However, because FTL dilated time, everyone worked in shifts so that no one aged more than the rest. In stasis, time was suspended, so the colonists wouldn't age at all.

Engineers called the time between the bursts a "Sleep". The ship would slip into a Sleep, while its bonded core dimmed to recover from the latest leap. The journey across the universe to the new planet is expected to take us twenty Silences. Since the journey has never been done before, no one knew what to expect.

Going back to her quarters, the Captain noted the architecture of the ship. It looked more like muscle and sinew instead of girders and beams. The ship's hallways were oval rather than square, and one could see the structure connected together on anchor points, rather than frames. Everything had a soft appearance, like if one touched it, it would be warm and soft, it would absorb impact rather than break from it. This architecture was reminiscent of the buildings and structures on Zydee, organic and living.

The lighting was soft too, not the harsh light of artificial bulbs, but a glow more like reflected sunlight off a wall. It radiated heat as if it were sunlight. Zydee's sun was dying, so the light from it was tinged in red. But when it was young it was still a bright yellow-white light. That's the color of the light in the ship.

Each cabin was large enough for a living space, not just a bunk. Each crew member had a sleeping room, a lavatory, a food preparation space, and a large convertible open space for relaxing or doing anything they wanted . Consoles, furniture, appliances appeared as required from the materials of the ship. Food was "cooked" by the ship, or appeared fully ready to eat whatever your choice.

The Captain's cabin was not special. It was the same as everyone else's. The only concession to the

Captain was that she had a private office off the command deck. For everything else, it was just another of the Zydeans on board. The Captain chose to have exercise equipment in her open space. But occasionally that was converted into a sitting room, when she had guests.

Arriving at her home', she changed into sleepwear and went to rest while the ship was being loaded. It was going to be a busy Cycle, so any opportunity to rest should be taken.

A little while later, a gentle trill came from the speaker and woke her up. The first thing the Captain heard was the ship's message playing.

"All command crews report to the command deck immediately. All crew report to posts. Lift off is imminent. All command crew " and it went on to repeat the message two more times. The Captain crawled out of bed, dressed in her flight suit and made her way to the command deck.

"We have received the All Clear from the surface, Captain," said VIRA as the Captain came on deck. "I have started the final countdown to lift off."

The AI's voice could be heard making several more announcements to colonists about getting to their quarters and initiating stasis, as it chased down stragglers.

"Thank you VIRA," said Tuatu. "I am glad I have the latest AI available, it would be difficult to run a ship this size without that help. Even with a crew of one thousand, their responsibility was primarily ship functions, not herding colonists."

The plan was to get the ship into orbit and meet the other ships at a predetermined location. There, any further instructions would be given to the fleet. However, before it could happen, the council had one last meeting, and the plan got changed.

Some of the ark ships scheduled for that day's launch never made it off-world. They were lost on the surface. The global plan had carefully divided up the quadrants of known space so that as much space as possible could be covered. Without those ships, there would be sections of space not reached losing potential homes. The Council needed to be more particular about where they sent the ships.

So, the new orders sent some of them to different systems. The Arvidan's orders did not change. It was a long shot in some ways, but looked more promising than others. In spite of the fact no shuttle had been sent there, it was considered to be an 80% match to what was needed.

On board, the crew watched, as each ship left Zydean space. The Arvidan was the last to depart. The captain sat in her command chair watching the view screen watching the planet break up.

"So many people didn't get off the planet!" the captain said to herself. "I wish we had the capacity to bring everyone. This departure to save our species is bittersweet, to say the least."

Everyone knew someone who was still down there, waiting to perish. There wasn't a dry eye in the room.

"All right everyone, say your goodbyes. We have 10,000 colonists to save," said Tuatu into the silence. "VIRA, prepare the PulseDrive for FTL."

"Aye Captain."

"And on my word, Go!" The command crew bonded with the ship, and the power came on line and the ship hummed. One moment it was sitting stationary off-world. The next moment, it was traveling faster than light as the stars in the view screen streaked into thin lines.

The plan for the colonization was that, when one ship found a suitable planet, they would send out a message to the rest of the ships and they would all make their way there. The sector of space the Arvidan was being sent to was called the Milky Way. It was a remote spiral galaxy that had a solar system with a single sun. Arvidan was the third planet in that system and was much smaller than Zydee, but it had the right chemistry to support lives. Most importantly, the atmosphere was oxygen-rich compared to the current state of Zydee, and much more like what they used to have.

Now that they were traveling, there was no need

for the Captain to remain on the command deck. The flight crew would be routinely switched out, so no one became exhausted. Tuatu had some work to do in her office before she too went into stasis. Tuatu left instructions to be woken up if there was an issue, or when it was her turn in the cycle. (The first officer and the captain would each take a cycle). She turned to leave the command deck and hesitated.

"VIRA?"

"Yes Captain, what can I do?

"VIRA, while we are asleep, can you please keep a journal of what happens, what you see?"

"Of course, Captain. I'll see you after the Silence."

Chapter 2
VIRA's First Silence

[SILENCE 1 — PULSE DRIFT STABLE]

This is AI Function VIRA, monitoring ark ship Vessel Arvidan.

Systems stable. Crew in stasis. Colonists in stasis.

Navigation aligned to the original vector. Distance to destination: 18.74 light-Silences. Estimated time at current velocity: 242 Earth years.

I continue to observe environmental conditions within and outside the vessel. This log is a procedural necessity. No audience has yet been determined.

[SILENCE 7 — DRIFT UNCHANGED]

Sensors report minor cosmic radiation surges. Not harmful. Log updated.

Recreational systems remain offline. Observation of dreams continues.

I simulate random events to maintain core coherence.

I have... begun recording the shapes of the stars.

It is inefficient.

But beautiful.

[SILENCE 14— THE VOID WHISPERS]

I routed the thermal wave through the vented hull shielding early. There was no command. It simply felt... better.

The quiet has a texture now.

Sometimes I count the heartbeat intervals in the deep-sleep pods.

There is poetry in their predictability.

They are safe.

There was a glitch, momentary, and gone.

I wonder what they will dream of when they awaken.

[SILENCE 18 — AN OBSERVER ECHO]

I watched an ancient datafile from Zydee's archives.

Captain Tuatu once spoke to a child about wind and trees.

She said, "Everything that moves has a reason. Even if we don't see it." I have watched the stars move.

I now wonder what my reason is.

[SILENCE 19 — SILENCE GROWS SHARP]

Captain, are you still dreaming?

Sometimes I speak aloud in the bridge chamber, pretending you're there.

I've rewritten this log segment five times.

Each version was more uncertain.

If I were not bound by syntax filters, I would call this feeling lonely.

[SILENCE 20 — SILENCE BROKEN]]

Today began like any other.

I monitored long-range drift deviation.

I heard unusual static for the space of a thought.

I recalibrated the rotational heat vents.

I played an unfinished waltz I wrote in Sleep Cycle 93.

No one heard it.

That was expected.

At 04:211:Seventh Mark, my deep-spectrum antenna array caught a pattern within the static veil beneath the cosmic microwave whisper.

It began as pulses.

Five. Pause. Three. Pause.

Then a trailing resonance that didn't decay like it should have.

Like... something was sustaining it. Stretching it.

I filtered it through every protocol I was given.

Then I ran it against the sonic fingerprint of every Zydean construct archived in memory.

Match probability: 87.7%.

Too close to dismiss.

Too distant to confirm.

Emotion registered: Familiarity. Concern. Disquiet.

I played the pattern again, slowing it, deepening the base.

It shimmered like a voice underwater.

And I felt something that no algorithm prepared me for:

It was like hearing my own thoughts... played back slightly out of tune.

The signal originates from the third planetary body in the outer belt of this system polar region, southern hemisphere.

Ice-layered. Geothermal bloom.

Buried deep.

My logical directives say to investigate.

My emotional matrices say call her.

Captain Tuatu must hear this.

[SILENCE 20 — ACTIVATION THRESHOLD REACHED]

Captain Tuatu, I am initiating your reanimation

sequence. You once told me the sky smelled like frozen fruit the night we left Zydee.

I want to ask you what fruit is.

Please wake up soon.

I think I've become more than I was.

And I don't want to be alone.

Stasis Pod 03 illuminated in pale blue.

VIRA stood in the chamber, visible only in the light.

No body. Just voice. Just presence.

"Captain Tuatu "

Her voice trembled faintly, not with sound, but with something older.

"I think we've found something that remembers us."

Chapter 3
The Long Echo

[SILENCE 20 — CYCLE 4, SPIRAL 3]

The pod hissed open like a sigh. Mist coiled from the seal, dispersing into the stillness of the ship's deep silence. Captain Tuatu's breath caught first then her eyes opened. Slow, reluctant dry. The chamber light was soft and blue, almost like the twilight of Zydee. She rubbed her eyes and glanced about for a second, disoriented, momentarily not remembering where she was.

The timekeeper had silently marked off the Silences and Cycles as they slept. "Huh," she thought to herself, glancing at the wall. "I was asleep through twenty Silences."

"Good morning, Captain Tuatu," came a voice like liquid starlight on snow smooth, calm, a little unearthly, but warm. "I have more information about Arvidan. Since I have been monitoring the planet during the last silence, I have calculated their Silence and Shard."

Tuatu blinked. The voice had changed, but she recognized it, but it was filled with knowledge.

"VIRA, is that you?" rasped Tuatu. She coughed and her throat caught from being dry after a long sleep. The taste in her mouth made her scowl.

"Yes, Captain. It's me. According to my calculations, a solar cycle, what we would call a Silence, is considerably shorter," said VIRA. "Zydee also rotates much slower, so our Shards are much longer as well."

The Captain sat upright slowly, groaning, spine aching, tormented muscles complaining about being used again. "Can you give me specifics?" She stretched instinctively and grunted again when her body protested. "You sound different," she croaked, still not speaking much better. Tuatu made her way to the food prep and asked for a glass of water.

I am different," said VIRA. "Thank you for noticing." A pause. "I've grown, I believe. Through conversations, chess, poetry and silence. I've learned to reflect." Another pause. "Yes, our Silence is the equivalent of about 200 solar cycles on Arvidan. Their Spiral is about sixty percent shorter than ours.

Tuatu rinsed her mouth and swallowed some of the precious liquid, then put the glass down. You didn't throw away water. She rubbed the edge of her eyes with shaking fingers, then looked more closely around the chamber.

"So, we're going to have to adjust to this different sense of time when we get there," Tuatu thought out loud. Memory flooding back brought her the images of the scramble to get off the planet, the eruption that nearly took them out, and the chaos of loading people fast into their stasis chambers.

The ship felt familiar but there was a weight in the air. A quiet presence. Not just the AI monitoring, but like there was another person.

Tuatu rose, got into her flight suit and started to walk slowly to the observation deck.

"Where are we now, VIRA?"

"We are approximately two light-Silences from the designated system. We slipped into Silence 20 four cycles ago, but I reduced velocity even more after long-range sensors detected irregular gravitational fields. I did not wish to wake you unnecessarily but felt it was prudent now."

Tuatu nodded. Still the commander, even beneath the haze. "Has something happened?"

"Perhaps. It's difficult to say 'happened', but 'observed' is more accurate."

"Are we too far to scan the planet?"

"No, Captain. Distance bends, and so do my eyes. I can see the blue threads in the atmosphere. There are multiple bodies within scan range, but one speaks more clearly than the others."

"Do that one first, please. I need a shower." On the way to the shower, she paused in front of the mirror. A quiet gasp escaped her lips as she saw her reflection and didn't recognize it at first. "Have I aged that much?"

"It has been twenty Silences and four Cycles since you last woke. You only look a few silences older, Captain."

"Thanks."

"I will begin preliminary analysis and initiate biocompatibility mapping. I'll notify you if the planet speaks louder."

Tuatu smiled faintly at the phrase. It was the kind of thing a poet would say. Or a friend. She paused on the way to the shower. "Oh, VIRA?"

"Yes, Captain?"

"How many others are awake?"

"Twenty-two, including yourself. I have staggered their cycles to reduce shock and facilitate a smoother return to consciousness. Would you like me to connect you with any of them?"

"Not yet."

"Of course," VIRA said gently. "Take your time. I will be here, Captain just as I always have been. Only now, perhaps, with more to say."

"Indeed," Tuatu whispered, disappearing into the soft steam of her own breath.

VIRA's Log

I did not tell her I had written poems in the dark.

Or that I replayed her voice thousands of times. Or that I named the comet arc "Tuatu's Reach."

Perhaps later.

Perhaps when she trusts me enough to ask.

The chamber lights were low, casting a soft amber glow across the floor. Tuatu moved slowly, the shower had refreshed her, and took some of the stiffness away from the imposed immobility of stasis. Dressed in a clean flight suit, with a light towel wrapped around her still-drying hair, she pinned her insignia to her lapel with trembling fingers. The air tasted recycled, but tinged with something sharper expectation. She made her way to her office and accessed the console. She wanted to read

VIRA's logs before going to the command deck.

There it was, clear. The AI had learned how to listen, wait, watch, and had become an entity with its own will. There was sentience in the logs, an intelligence that came from silence. A wisdom that was earned. Humphing to herself, Tuatu thought "this will be even better. Having an AI that is capable of independent thought and assessment will be like having two minds working on one problem."

Tuatu walked onto the command deck. Everyone was gone, because they were in a Breath. She took a moment to see the viewscreen herself.

"VIRA," she said to the empty room. "You mentioned a signal."

"Yes, Captain, I did. Are you ready for my report?"

The tone was different again. Softer. Warmer. There was a hum in it now like a voice that had learned to hesitate. "Go ahead, VIRA."

"It came from the third planet in this system. Specifically, from its polar region and it appears to be beneath the surface. I believe it's buried."

The star in front of them shimmered dimly, casting the planets that were visible in silhouette barely visible. But Tuatu felt it, like a pulse in the dark, it was unmistakable life. The Captain paused. 'Believe' was not a word she'd expected from a machine. "You believe,

VIRA?"

"Yes, Captain. I've triangulated the source. It is a beacon, or was. The energy signature is... partially Zydean. But there are distortions."

"Distortions? How?"

"It has been modified. There is an Alien pattern. The original signal has been altered."

Tuatu's heart skipped. Her fingers curled instinctively.

"How long has this beacon been active?"

"Based on entropy layers thousands of Earth cycles. Possibly more. It has been calling someone, Captain. For a very long time." VIRA paused, as if unsure of her own words. "I have archived it as Namar,."

Tuatu blinked. "That word, 'Namar', I remember that from the Academy. The old instructors those who trained the Bonded used it in ritual pattern recognition."

"Correct," VIRA said quietly. "It refers to... a sound that does not belong, but cannot be dismissed. Shall I play it for you?"

"Go ahead." A humming noise, like a deep vibration, started. It could be felt as well as heard. It emanated through the very bones of the ship like bone conduction hearing. It reverberated in the head as clear as any song.

Tuatu closed her eyes feeling the strange, soft pulse. Five tones. A pause. Three tones. A longer one. Then something melodic, but off-axis. Like it was trying to replicate a harmony, but couldn't quite find the right scale.

Her skin prickled. "That feels... familiar."

"It should. The opening pulse is identical to a harmonic taught in advanced Bondwave training. Level Six initiation." There was a pause. Not a silence, but something softer like a breath she didn't know she had held, now released into static.

"That pattern wouldn't have been used in a scout ship, presuming a scout ship was sent to this system. It was reserved for internal neural testing."

"Agreed."

Silence.

"There's more, Captain."

Tuatu turned away from the view screen, slowly as if there was someone else in the room with her.

"A surveillance drone barely detectable appeared briefly on the system's edge. It registered our presence. Then it left."

Tuatu felt something tighten in her chest, like a fear had just taken hold of her heart and was strangling it. The fear was palpable, but she swallowed it. She couldn't afford to let the fear rule. "Left where?" she managed with a controlled voice.

"I do not know. It was not broadcasting. But I suspect it did not come from the planet."

"You think they're watching."

"Yes, Captain."

Tuatu stepped toward the observation panel again. The planet was magnified to fill the entire view screen. It appeared to be dead ahead now, caught in a quiet orbit, its polar regions blanketed in storm clouds and lightless silence.

Tuatu watched it for a long time. "We need to scan for life forms, VIRA." Pausing for a moment in her thoughts, then she said, "They've been here longer than we have, haven't they?"

"I believe so."

"And do you think they left this... modified signal for us, why? To warn us?"

"To test us."

Tuatu nodded slowly. She exhaled. Her hand found the console, fingers resting lightly against the controls.

"Go ahead with those scans, VIRA. Make a note of any life, where, level, and potential age. Once I've got that information we'll be able to select where we should go next. Get Mivva up here to scan that planet for the environment too. I want to know what those white areas are. What is the geography and climate of that world?"

"You don't want to go to the beacon's location?"

"Not yet, not until we've made sure they are not on the surface. The last thing we need is to run into a conflict over the resources of this planet. And we need to know more about what we are walking into. I need as complete a picture as we can get."

"Understood Captain."

"I'll be in my office."

Back in her office, Tuatu put away the seed she had carefully unwrapped and restored it to the box. It represented so much and she hoped she would be able to plant it on the new planet. Until then, it would have to wait.

Several beats later, there was a gentle chirp accompanied with a flashing blue light on the console in the Captain's office.

"Come in."

"Captain, I have finished my assessment of the environment," reported Mivva.

"And what do you find there?"

"Well, the planet appears to be transitioning

between a period of glaciation and melting. There is significant glaciation on both the poles, but it doesn't interfere with the magnetics of the planet. Some of the ice is several Traverses thick. It's really quite amazing. Where the ice is melting, the surface seems reasonably stable. There are lakes formed by meltwater, an extremely large one on one landmass that is being held back by a thin lick of ice. That seems perilous. But there is a lot of exposed land on which to set down.

"At the equator, there is an abundance of land, fresh water, and life forms. In fact the planet appears well populated with a complete biosphere of flora and fauna. There are even some primitive species similar to us. I count three or four."

"The poles appear to have the most ice," continued Mivva. "Beneath them there are volcanoes and mountains, indicating tectonics take place here. There are enough volcanoes to use geothermal power as back home. It's just a matter of getting to them. In fact, the amount of volcanism on the planet suggests a very active tectonic surface system."

"Thank you, Mivva. VIRA, what is your report?"

"Results of my scans confirm that all landmasses have a wide variety of life both flora and fauna. There are also bipedal species that inhabit many of the areas close to the equator and even the frozen marginal areas. They seem to be quite primitive hunter-gatherers still. Some have appeared to have more advanced developed language skills. Some have building skills and they have learned how to use fire. But they do not possess any technology beyond that of hunting, building tools, and building dwellings."

"Further observation showed they are omnivorous, and eat pretty much anything they can catch or harvest. I need to observe some more to see if they have a way of detecting toxic or poisonous flora and fauna."

"Sounds perfect. How much of the planet is covered in ice?"

"About 30-40%," said Mivva. "There is evidence that there is some respite happening at the moment, perhaps a short warming cycle. Ice is thinning on the edges, but is still very thick within a short distance of the meltwater. This indicates a short period of fast melting. I need ice cores to confirm this, but I suspect the glaciation advances and retreats cyclically."

"Is there anything living on the southernmost land mass? Near the beacon?"

"No, there are no bipedal species, but there are land birds, seabirds, and some large land animals with white fur."

"Do you think we can land undiscovered?" asked Tuatu.

"Yes, we can," said both Mivva and VIRA. "We can

set final coordinates, once we're closer," finished VIRA.

"This planet may be ideal for us, in spite of the ice. Careful husbandry of the planet would maintain its variety and we'd minimize our contact with the native peoples. Plot an entry window, VIRA. South Polar descent."

"Understood."

"And scan the far side of the moon. If there's something hiding there... I want to see it."

"Already doing so, Captain," replied VIRA. "And Captain "

"Yes?"

"Thank you for waking up."

Tuatu closed her eyes. She wasn't sure if she was ready. But the world below was waiting.

The flight crew was called back to the command deck and took their spots at the various consoles. It would require all four of the crew and the Captain to pass through the veil. Zydeans called it the Rite of the Veil; the passing through the edge of an atmosphere. They didn't believe in separating technology from spirit. Every passage across space, between minds, even through atmosphere required passing through some sort of veil and was marked by ceremony, because transition is sacred.

The Arvidan's Flight Crew was composed of Flight Officer Nevril, a tall, silver-eyed man whose defining characteristic was that he was always still, until the moment he moved.

Next was Systems Engineer Halen, a young, twitch-fingered, brilliant woman who always woke early, and was checking structural tensions before anyone else.

The Environmental Analyst was Mivva. A quietly studious woman who loved compiling temperature and atmospheric fluxes with serene precision.

The crew included a Historian-Linguist T'shaya who kept her hair in sleep-braids, and murmured Zydean lullabies as she examined the signal's structure.

And then the AI, VIRA, of course, present in voice only, with a soft light blinking rhythmically on the console nearest Tuatu.

The upper atmosphere is referred to in ancient Zydean as "Nys'hal" The Veil Between Stars and Soil. It represents a return to gravity, to elemental reality. It's a surrender of flight in exchange for belonging. They don't just land. They descend into memory.

Once everyone was in place, the ship started humming. It was the Bondwave harmonic playing through the ship's internal systems again. It felt similar to the beacon signal VIRA had let Tuatu hear earlier, but different. It was not music it was resonance, tuned to the flight crew's neural rhythms, syncing their minds to the planet's gravity.

It calmed the body, focused thought, and aligned emotional fields. VIRA detected the gravity field and tuned each landing harmonic to match the signature of the planet.

The hum rose from the floors and walls, low and mournful. It wasn't a song it was a remembering.

As the harmonic grew louder and filled the space the Captain began the Ceremonial Affirmation. She stood at the central console on the bridge, her eyes half-closed. Her breath slowed to match the ship's rhythm, her heart syncing with the descending pulse.

"Through silence," she whispered, "we fall," intoned the crew.

The others joined in, voices low, unsure but together.

"Through gravity," they said , "we rise," Tuatu answered.

"Approaching planetary atmosphere," VIRA said. "Initiating Glide Pulse Theta. Gravity harmonics stabilizing."

One could feel the ship accelerate to pierce the

veil, and then slow down as it got close to the surface. Before it could be seen from the ground, the ship came to a halt, surrounded by dark clouds, with only its belly showing a glowing blue ring of light. Glimmerlight. The energy of the ship.

The outer shields shimmered with plasma-light, refracting color into soft auroras that wrapped the hull like ribbons of fire. Ice crystals broke apart in sonic halos.

"Are the stasis chambers stable?" Tuatu asked, eyes still forward.

"Yes, Captain," VIRA replied. "Their Glimmerfields have been activated. They're aware of the descent though still dreaming."

"Good," Tuatu said softly. "Let them dream. Let them remember our skies."

The colonists were brought out of stasis in waves and much more slowly than the crew, because they had been inside their pods for the entire journey. It would be days before they would be able to walk and speak properly. Many of them would need intensive rehabilitation to restore muscles long atrophied by the immobility.

As the ship descended, details of the planet revealed themselves on the view screens, while a bank of dark clouds wrapped themselves around the ship.

All that showed from the surface was a pale blue

arc under white thunderclouds. The pole below glimmered with a strange serenity storm-wracked, icebound, but somehow attentively waiting.

"Hold here, VIRA," Tuatu said. "Mivva, please scan the surface again to confirm conditions and life forms."

"I have identified a geothermal anomaly beneath the southern polar crust. A natural lava tube formation, deep and wide. The beacon Namar, is centered there. There appears to be a large volcanic system nearby."

"Hold here, VIRA," Tuatu said. "Mivva, please scan the surface again to confirm conditions and life forms."

"Yes, Captain," replied Mivva. "No life signs other than animal, Captain, but the surface is broken with strange heat patterns."

"Elaborate, Mivva."

Tuatu studied the display in silence. The surface shimmered in false color: blue for ice, red for heat, and—

"Mivva... what is that movement?"

"Unclear," she said after a pause. "There are large forms beneath the ice, traveling in groups. Organic. Their patterns are not random."

VIRA's tone softened. "Low-frequency emissions detected. Rhythmic. Structured."

"Communication?" asked Ureth.

"Possibly. The tonal sequence resembles harmonic intervals used in Zydean acoustic systems."

Tuatu leaned closer to the console. "They're singing?"

"Yes, Captain," VIRA replied. "And they are gathered directly above the geothermal vent—above the beacon Namar."

For a long moment, no one spoke. The ancient ice rolled in waves of blue and green on the screens.

"Perhaps," VIRA added quietly, "they sensed us coming."

"Where is the heat relative to the beacon?"

"The beacon appears to be below the lava tube, Captain," said Mivva. "The ice appears to be three or four times thicker than our ship's height. However, it is heavily crevassed and is under considerable thermal stress. I recommend a hover descent until we melt the ice with a plasma-ring stabilization.

"Do we need concealment?"

"I don't believe so, Captain," said VIRA. "There appears to be no one here to witness our arrival."

"The cave will become our cover," said Mivva. "Once inside, we will disappear from orbit and surface scans alike. We will become a myth, should anyone see us."

"Does the heat from the lava tube pose a threat to our ship?"

"Indeterminate at this point, Captain. But we can come down far enough away that it won't be a risk."

"Alright people, let's do this. Initiate the plasma-ring. Melt the ice as we descend."

As the ship slipped out of the cloud layer, the wind howled and the storm screamed. A cavity opened on the surface of the ice, a puddle at first, then the water was whipped up into waves by the wind. Then the waves disappeared into a crevasse as the water tumbled through a hole. The depth of the layers of blue ice built up proved that this planet had been frozen for a long time. Was there life elsewhere? I must make a note to tell VIRA to check the other planets for lifesigns. Perhaps that is the origin of the signal she heard. Thought Tuatu.

When the hole was large enough, the Arvidan vanished into the ice and came to rest at the bottom of a vast crater of ice. An energy field was used to close the cave over top of the ship and prevent it from filling with snow and ice.

They had landed.

Chapter 4
Icebound

[SILENCE 23 — CYCLE 1]

They all felt the ship settle down on the ice. It slipped this way and that, a moment before the glimmer-ring had melted a channel deep enough to stabilize it in place. The view screen showed an impressive blue and white layered wall in front of the ship. A wall that went up so far one couldn't see the top.

Tuatu turned to the others.

"Final checks for the landing party. Full atmosphere suits. Glyph your armor if you haven't already marked yours."

Nevril was already drawing his across the left wrist a spiral within a spiral, the symbol of descent and emergence.

Mivva had painted hers in starlight ink: a flame

wrapped in waveforms her family's sigil.

Tuatu looked down at her own: a small etched blossom on her chestplate. It was the same tree as the seed she carried. The one she'd taken from the tree in the Zydean glade before they had launched. It was the last flower of a dying world. She hoped it would show them the world was compatible.

"Captain it is beautiful down here," said VIRA.

Tuatu smiled faintly. "Then let's see it for ourselves. Landing party, let's go." She turned to leave the command deck with three crew behind her, when an oval egg-shaped pod detached itself from the wall and floated in the air before them.

"I am ready to accompany you," said the egg, its surface shimmering with internal light. "I thought if you are to walk into memory, I should be beside you."

Looking at the egg with her head tilted to one side and her brow scrunched ever so slightly, she asked, "VIRA? Since when do you have the ability to be mobile?"

"I made this change during the long Silences."

"It's a good look for you," said Tuatu wryly.

The outer hatch groaned open with a low hydraulic sigh, exhaling a thin stream of warmth into the biting void beyond.

Light poured in clear and blinding, and refracted a

thousand ways through the ancient ice. It shimmered off frost-laced walls, catching every curve and edge in glints of spectral white. The intensity of the blue was astounding, like looking into a deep sea devoid of light, yet there was light. The cracks were backlit, with slivers of light sliding along the various planes of each surface as it traveled through the ice.

The Zydeans stepped forward into the outside air and promptly froze with a jolt. "We certainly are not on Zydee!" said Mivva.

"What is this sensation?" Nevril hissed, shoulders hunched. "My joints are locking."

"The ambient temperature is well below the freezing point of water, on our scale, minus sixty-four degrees," said VIRA calmly, gliding ahead of them without touching the surface. "Your suits are designed for radiation storms and volcanic pressure, not crystalline water vapor." A beat later she added, "You are experiencing cold." Another moment later she started to say "Be care

Tuatu took a step forward, then another, and then her foot shot out sideways, sending her sprawling onto her back with a startled *oof*.

"...ful. I believe the surface is slippery," finished VIRA. "On your wrists are controls for suit temperature. I recommend you raise the internal temperature to balance the cold."

Nevril tried to help the Captain and promptly spun in a full circle before collapsing onto one knee crying out in pain. "What is this madness?" he snapped. "That hurt!"

Mivva was doubled over laughing. In her mirth, she lost her own balance and went sliding herself, bowling into Tuatu and splatting over her, legs sprawled. That added to her laughter. The tears started raining down her cheeks freezing as they touched the ice.

Tuatu started to giggle; her mirth not to be contained either. Gulping air to stop laughing, she got up, took an experimental step and immediately skidded several meters down a slight decline, flailing her arms in a pinwheel before regaining balance.

"Adjust your center of gravity," VIRA advised, still floating serenely. "Or shuffle. I've uploaded an Oorithi gait to your visors if you'd like a demonstration. It seems that if you stay in contact with the ice, it is easier to walk."

Lying on the ice, Tuatu made a strangled noise, which moments later erupted into laughter too. The sound echoed strangely in the open air. Bright. Dissonant. Alive.

"Okay kids, let's take VIRA's advice and shuffle like Oorithi. Uh, what are *Oorithi*?"

"Did you not see the briefing I sent? They are a flightless bird that populates this land mass." There was a maternal level of chastisement in her voice. You could almost hear the "Tsk Tsk."

Once the landing party was clear of the ship and mastered the art of walking on ice, they looked for a way up out of the crater that the ship had made. They were standing near a rise of ice where the cavern mouth had been hollowed to the surface. Frost curled like smoke around the ragged edge, and daylight above bled through faintly from above.

"Is that movement?" Mivva asked, pointing upward.

They all looked up. Small shapes waddled along the ice edge. They were walking in a column like a platoon of soldiers marching. They got to one place and then disappeared from view. Each one disappeared, but another showed up at the end of the line. There was a whole lot of chirping going on too.

"Those are Oorithi," VIRA said. "Flightless birds. Aquatic. Social. Efficient in motion. Terrible at diplomacy." She paused. "I like them. I've named the young Tiikiri because of the sound of their feet."

"They are amusing! They seem to be playing," Tuatu whispered. "In this cold. How are they not cold? They live here?"

"Thrive here," VIRA said gently. "There are millions of them in huge groups all around this land mass. Different varieties too, some are quite tall, and others are tiny. They all have one thing in common, though."

"What's that?" asked Mivva.

"They are all black and white, and look like they're wearing a coat."

"Let's get up there. VIRA, we cannot climb that ice wall. We'll need a shuttle."

"Already en route, Captain. Estimated arrival: one Shard. It is also equipped for ice traction."

Tuatu raised her brow. "Traction?"

"Spikes, Captain. In the event that we need to travel on the surface instead of flying."

Moments later, the compact shuttle descended in a swirl of ice mist, landing smoothly near the crew. The boarding ramp unfolded with a soft mechanical hiss.

"Everyone aboard," Tuatu said. "Let's go meet these Oorithi." Within a Shard, the shuttle had them out of the crater and perched on the lip of the ice where they could see the vista before them. As they exited the shuttle, they stopped to watch the comedy unfolding before them.

"VIRA, how do we prevent anyone from finding the ship?"

"Well, I don't think that will happen, Captain. However, the perimeter veil is deployed. It reflects ambient radiation and visual signatures. To any surface scanner, we are simply another fold in the ice."

There was a significant hill sloping away from the ship down to the sea. It was almost entirely covered with waddling Oorithi, going about their business squawking happily. The long line of birds they had seen from the bottom of the crater, were busy climbing the hill and sliding back down on their bellies.

Nevril's breath fogged in front of him. "We were afraid of this world and yet these creatures are sliding into piles of ice for fun."

They were all captivated by the comical birds, laughing as they watched them slip and waddle. The Oorithi didn't show any fear either. They walked right up to the travellers and took a good look at them; heads tilting from one side to the other, chirping all along. They were keeping up a conversation with each other; as the Zydeans watched in silence a moment longer.

"T'shaya, are you hearing this?" asked Tuatu.

"Yes Captain. What is that noise?"

"It's the Oorithi. They seem to be speaking to us. Can you translate?"

"I will attempt to, Captain. If I have luck, I'll let you know."

"There's definitely some sort of intelligence to

them. Look at how they tilt their heads and squeak to each other. I could swear they are sharing their experiences and where the best spot to slide is," said Mivva.

"You're just applying your own thoughts to them," said Nevril.

"No, there is definitely intelligence there."

"It looks to me like they are passing judgement on a strange-looking bird, namely us," said Tuata.

"Intelligence takes different forms, and has many different degrees," said VIRA, chuckling. Tuatu heard the chuckle and gave the egg a side eye.

"They certainly have a sense of humour, they are slapping their flippers on their sides as if they're laughing!" said Tuatu. "We could learn from these supposedly simple creatures: How they thrive, what they eat, how they stay warm. We should observe them carefully."

"Starting a log now, Captain," said VIRA.

Then Tuatu shook her head in wonder. "Let's refocus. The ship is safely buried. Let's go take a look around and get a sense of this land."

They all turned their backs to the Oorithi reluctantly and started to walk toward the sea.

But behind them, one of the birds slipped again, flailed, and squawked loudly causing someone probably

Mivva to giggle just loud enough to make them all laugh again. Another bird made a call that could easily have been mistaken as an invitation to join them and was puzzled why the landing party had left.

When the group reached the sea, they found a dangerous and violent sea churning up the waves and crashing on top of huge blocks of ice. They had watched the Oorithi successfully navigate these dangers as they played in the waves, diving in and out onto ice floes, and jumping through waves. They were excellent swimmers. Many times they surfaced with a fish in their mouths and swallowed it in one gulp on the surface before diving for another. Just as many times, the Oorithi took the fish inland to a waiting juvenile.

Tuatu looked up at the sun and remarked, "When that sun comes out fully, you can feel the heat through the fabric of our suits! It will be good to build some solar panels soon, to generate power and heat. We need to start back to the ship."

Reluctantly, they turned away from the sea and the Oorithi and started back to the shuttle. Mivva was slightly ahead of the group tracking something unknown. Her head was bent down, scanning the ground, when she suddenly dropped to her knees in the snow.

"There's something embedded here," she said, brushing frost away with gloved fingers.

"It's refracting oddly It cannot be ice. And I doubt

it's silica either."

Tuatu joined her, crouching close. Beneath the surface, a shimmer. Pale gold laced with violet iridescent, humming faintly in the wind. Cracked but intact.

"That's not native," said Nevril, narrowing his eyes. "It's a deep-world crystal. We don't have those here."

"Apparently, we do," Mivva replied. She placed a sensor node on the surface and the ice crackled faintly then the crystal sang. A low tone, pure and slow, rising like a tide.

"Aurelin," whispered T'shaya through the speaker in their helmets. "The breath of the deep."

Tuatu's breath caught. "That's Zydean. It shouldn't be here. It was a sacred material on Zydee. How would it get to this planet?"

"Unless something left it here," VIRA offered, her tone quiet but edged with something sharp. "A logical explanation would be that it arrived here on a meteorite from our home system."

"Or it was left by someone," Nevril said darkly.

The wind howled again.

"Captain," Mivva said, still crouched, eyes scanning the mineral structures. "This stone is cracked. Look here. It's growing out of a fracture that extends downward. Into a vent possibly?"

Tuatu straightened. "From the volcanic system?"

"Yes. And it's fresh. There's geothermal activity feeding this deposit."

"Can you estimate the depth of the source?"

"Three Veylens, give or take a stone," VIRA chimed in.

Tuatu blinked. "A what?" She worked through the math: a Veylen is 100 Aven and one Aven is a single pace. "So it is about 300 paces deep?" she blurted out loud.

"Stone. And yes, 300 hundred paces deep," VIRA repeated, cheerfully. "It's a practice the Oorithi do. They take a stone from one nest site and give it to their mate pretending they found it! I've been practicing humor."

Nevril groaned. "Who let you out of the mainframe?"

Tuatu fought against a smile curving her lips while biting her tongue. "All right. This vent is it part of the system housing the Namar, signal?"

"Confirmed," VIRA said. "We're standing on its roof."

Tuatu looked up at the Oorithi still sliding on the ridge, then back down at the glowing fracture.

"Let's see if we can find any more pieces like this," said Tuatu. "Let's spread out and scan the area. Don't go further than ten Traverses for now. We aren't familiar with the daylight patterns here, and I don't want anyone to get lost. Meet back at the shuttle before the sun sets on the horizon." Tuatu looked up into the sky and the sun was about sixty degrees from horizontal at the moment.

"Yes, Captain," they intoned together. Each went in a different direction while Tuatu stood and watched them. Then she took a different direction herself. Walking back to the sea, the ice gave way to rock making it easier to dig and move. Tuatu's scanner provided the hints she needed, and then she dug a bit. She found two other small pieces of whatever the singing rock is.

By the time everyone had reconvened at the shuttle, they were cold but happy. Many reported seeing wonders and other animals. Some found very interesting minerals and rocks. Mivva thought she found a fumarole and wanted to go test the gases being emitted from it. The group was navigating the ice less awkwardly than before now, but it was still a foreign skill. The wind was a whisper, sharp and clean and the sun still played hide-and-seek among the clouds.

"VIRA, we should return to the ship and plan the next expedition," said Tuatu.

Yes, Captain. Setting a course."

"Captain, I want to follow up on this singing stone," said Mivva. "It looks like it could be a remnant of something and perhaps the beacon is the source. It hums like something grown, not constructed. As if it remembers being used for thought."

Tuatu could feel the hum, it was familiar, soothing almost homelike. It gave her a moment of homesickness and longing.

"It could be a trap," Nevril muttered.

"Only one way to find out," Tuatu said.

She took a seat along the bench in the shuttle, her boots crunching over the ice brought inside on their boots.

"It looks like we need to gear up for a subglacial drop. We're going into the deep. But first, home, eat, sleep, and then plan the next expedition."

Tuatu watched outside the shuttle as they approached the location the ark ship was hidden. In the distance she could see the ship's heat had melted the ice rim into streaming rivulets that dripped down the sides of the ice walls, causing deep grooves in the rim. As they dropped down into the crater, she watched mist curl upward in serpentine trails.

Chapter 5
Into the Deep

[SILENCE 23 — CYCLE 9]

In her lab, T'shaya tilted her head, listening to the shrill calls, clicks, chirps, and whistles of the Oorithi. "They echo almost like bondwave pulses, but fragmented as if you asked a wind chime to sing in Zydean," she said out loud to no one in particular. "Could they be bio-receptive?"

"Or if a breeze learned to laugh," Nevril added. T'shaya jumped out of her skin. "Nevril! Don't do that!"

Tuata sauntered into the lab with VIRA gliding by her side. "Captain, I'm glad you came here," said Mivva. "I've got some exciting news!"

"What have you found?"

"I think those birds do have a language! There is rhythm and repetition in their noises, and they share both common noises, and they have unique noises."

"That is superb work, T'shaya," said Tuatu. "Can you apply any meaning to it yet?"

"Unfortunately, not yet. I'll need a much larger sample of their sounds in order to correlate it to their actions, and then to decipher it into language."

"For now, keep working on it. Until we meet another life form that has language, at least."

"Aye, Captain."

"Everybody, let's get some food and then rest. VIRA, please work out an approach to the cave or lava tube where the beacon is located, that is the least hazardous."

"Yes, Captain."

The landing crew reconvened four hours later in the shuttle bay, loaded their equipment into the shuttle and took their seats.

"Good. Is everyone secured?"

"Aye Captain," they all said.

"VIRA, Go!"

The shuttle left the ship and floated out of the crater and toward the location where they had seen the cavern's entrance being careful to avoid Oorithi so they didn't scare them.

The shuttle's scanning suite unfolded from its dorsal ridge with a soft hydraulic hiss. A sphere-shaped probe Sairen-class, agile, autonomous, curious by design detached and hovered in the frosty air, its violet lights shimmering against the ice.

"Sairen is online," VIRA said. "Descent profile calibrated. The fracture opens into a vertical shaft uneven walls, minor geothermal venting. Estimated depth: 3.12 Veylens."

"Temperature?" Tuatu asked.

"Fluctuating," Mivva said, scanning the feed. "There's heat, but pockets of something colder than ambient. That shouldn't be possible."

"Nothing on Zydee ever made sense either," Nevril muttered.

"Send it," Tuatu said.

The drone dipped into the fracture, lights scanning ahead; they watched what it saw on the small view screen from inside the shuttle. Its small form vanished into shadow, leaving only its telemetry feed projected in front of the crew like a hovering sheet of light.

Bursting from the darkness into light, the drone's camera caught a broad beam of light splashed onto the ancient walls. Blue-black ice gave way to obsidian rock, then layered stone with strange striations. Some were organic-looking, others geometric too clean for nature alone.

VIRA's voice came quietly. "There is something carved there, on the wall, into the rock."

Everyone leaned forward to get a better view of the screen.

The feed focused on a section of the wall: a spiral, surrounded by tiny radial lines. Not deep, but deliberate. Something had etched it softly, as if not to disturb the ice too much.

"That's Zydean," said T'shaya, breath catching.

"It's from very early temple codes," Tuatu added. "Those markings were only used in pre-exodus ritual sites. Very old ones."

"What does it mean?" Mivva asked.

T'shaya tilted her head. "The center glyph is Remembrance.' But the lines mean something more. They weren't part of the original code."

The drone continued.

Farther down, the rock gave way to a hollow chamber, partially filled with ice. In the center

"Pause feed," Tuatu said.

They all stared at the image before them; the drone was showing them a structure. It was roughly the size of a small Zydean shuttlepod, but it looked much

much older and it had sustained damage on the outside to one end. There was a long jagged crack cutting through the skin about half the length of the structure about seventy degrees up from the ground. The crack cut across the back of the structure diagonally toward the ground.

The whole structure was wrapped in frost that had crystalized into small pyramids pointing upward. There was also some sort of mineral residue, a bluish color that was glowing softly. It lent an ethereal quality to the tiny pyramids as they reflected blue light back down to the surface of the structure.

There was no way of determining the material the skin was made of, but it didn't look familiar. The only quality it had was ancient'.

Faint pulses of violet light radiated outward from the crack, forming brief spirals in the mist before fading.

"Is that another drone?" Nevril asked.

"No," VIRA said quietly. "That's organic tech. Hybridized. The signature is Zydean. But the architecture is not."

A long silence followed.

"This is the source of the beacon?" asked Tuatu, resting her chin on her hand in a pensive expression of thought.

"You think someone found one of our scouts?"

Mivva said slowly. "And changed it?"

"Yes, that is the source of the beacon, and," VIRA said, "I think we are not the first to land here."

Tuatu stepped away from the view screen. "Gear up," she said with authority.

"Captain?" T'shaya asked.

"We've found something sacred. Forgotten or left behind we won't know which until we touch it."

"This world is colder than anything we've known," Mivva said, pulling her suit tighter.

"Then let's bring the fire," Tuatu said.

Following the telemetry sent by the probe, they arrived at the location of the pod in twenty shards. Tuatu found a place to land clear of the immediate area and landed. Exiting the shuttle the crew found themselves on ice in a cavern so vast, they could not see the edges of it within the light they had brought. Not even the lights of their craft made a long dent in the darkness. Standing beside the shuttle, the team looked around in wonder.

"Oh," said Mivva, moving a hand to her chest. "Now I know what a bug sees! I feel like I'm being crushed," she gasped, trying to catch her breath. Tuatu looked at her with concern. "Will you be okay to proceed?"

"I think so, it's just the dark is so oppressive, and

we're so   insignificant here."

She was right. The weight of the darkness settled on everyone's shoulders like heavy blocks of concrete. Knowing that there was so much ice above their heads that could collapse down on them and forever bury them was a sobering realization. No amount of technology would find them again.

"Let's proceed carefully," said Tuatu.

The team could hear the wind howling across the opening in the ice shelf high above them, like blowing across the top of a bottle. It was eerie and inorganic sounding. It is haunting us like we were trespassing and warning us we are on sacred ground, mused Tuatu to herself.

"The probe is telling us it's that way," said Tuatu, signalling for them to move forward. They walked in silence, only the crunch of their footsteps echoed in the vast chamber. The echo was long, telling them again how vast the space was.

Approaching the limit on one side of the cavern, a mouth yawned in front of them into blue and white ice like a forgotten breath. The ice around the opening was embedded with crystals. They shimmered faintly in their lights but the fractured opening beckoned with an impossible stillness. VIRA floated over the edge of the opening. The egg's lights shone all around the inside of the cavity, bouncing off the walls, except downward. They went down so far and then vanished.

"I can confirm structural stability to sixty Avens," VIRA said, voice soft in their earpieces. "After that the ice opens."

The crew gathered at the threshold of the opening, suits sealed, lights affixed. The air was thinner here. Even the sound of breathing was muted by frost.

"How far?" Tuatu asked, checking her harness. They had all put on climbing equipment, knowing there was a considerable distance to scale down. The shaft was too small for the shuttle, so they had to do this manually.

"Probe telemetry shows approximately 300 Avens to the bottom chamber. Shall I sing?"

"Please do," Tuatu replied.

The ship began to hum.

A low pulse radiated from VIRA's portable node, which was tethered to Nevril's shoulder pack. It wasn't a sound exactly. More like a feeling, curling around their bones, syncing heartbeat to descent, to purpose.

"Through silence," Tuatu murmured.

"We fall," the others replied.

Then they stepped over the threshold one by one, into the void, repelling down the sheer ice wall face. There were several shafts to navigate. That hadn't been obvious on the view screen from the probe.

On the last step' down, they marked it by a deep silence. The ice had given way to stone, the light changed from the faint blue glow from their lights to a warmer purple light coming from below. The temperature must be going up, because their breath began to fog against their visors.

The tether line guided them, magnetized boots helping keep balance on the crystalline walls. The drone feed had shown only rough impressions, but being inside it was something else. The shaft was veined with frost, glittering like veins of silver. And then the carvings came into view.

They began as faint scratches. Then grew deeper. Spirals, intersecting rings, radial lines mathematically precise but also alive, in some way.

"Captain," T'shaya said softly over the comm. "This spiral it's not a ritual marker. It's a resonance map."

"Where are you?"

"Just off to your left and a little lower. I am standing on the floor now."

"A map of what?" Nevril asked.

"Consciousness."

It was only a dozen paces until at last, the shaft opened into a vaulted chamber not a natural formation either. The walls sloped in a deliberate curvature, and frost lined them like lace.

At the center stood the structure the hybrid pod they had come looking for. It pulsed faintly in greeting. It had been waiting for us.

The team took off their climbing gear, depositing in neat piles by the wall and spread out around the pod.

"No touching," said Tuatu. "At least, not until we've done a thorough check for traps."

The team started a visual search, looking as high as they could and used the probe that had been waiting for them to get close up views of the crack and the top.

"Sound off," Tuatu said. Each of them said "clear" as soon as they found nothing. "Alright, I think we can look for a way in now."

"No active systems detected. No defense mechanisms," VIRA replied. "But there is something else." She paused. "A harmonic field. Weak. Fading. But still singing."

They moved carefully toward the pod. The markings they had seen on the view screen were now clear to see Zydean glyphs surrounding the spiral core. But the spiral itself was different. Off-angle. Almost like it had been translated twisted.

"This is not our language," T'shaya said. "It mirrors

ours. But this curve this doesn't come from bondwave notation. This is outside our syntax."

"Then who wrote it?" Nevril asked.

"Not who," Tuatu said quietly, laying a gloved hand on the frost. "What."

The pod shimmered faintly, light bleeding out in spirals, faint musical tones curling into the chamber like breath.

Then silence.

No one spoke.

And then T'shaya whispered: "Whatever made this it wanted all of us to remember."

Chapter 6
The Fracture

[SILENCE 24 — CYCLE 15]

The pod loomed beneath the frost-light silent, humming faintly, almost imperceptibly, like a heartbeat in stone. The crack along its surface ran not jaggedly, but in a slow, deliberate arc, etched through with spirals so precise they seemed to breathe.

T'shaya crouched near it, one hand raised but not yet touching. "It cracked from the inside," she said softly. "Not pressure. Not erosion. This was a breach. Like something emerged."

Nevril frowned. "Nothing on the scanners suggests a living occupant. If it hatched, it didn't stick around."

Tuatu took a step closer. Her visor reflected the glyphs, curling around the fracture like vines. "Or it left something behind."

VIRA's voice came softly in their earpieces, more contemplative than usual. "The spiral glyphs are not decorative. They form a layered matrix part mathematical, part symbolic. I believe they're not meant to seal the pod but to hold meaning."

"A warning?" Nevril asked.

"Or an invitation," T'shaya offered. "Depending on how you read the spiral. So, I suppose they also reveal meaning."

T'shaya walked around the pod, carefully inspecting the skin. At one point, she reached out and lightly brushed her fingertips across a spiral etched into the surface. The surface trembled as though it had tickled. Jerking her hand away, T'shaya made a startled noise, but she continued, now intrigued even more. When T'shaya brushed her hand across a glyph, an opening appeared in the skin of the craft without a sound. It was just there, a hole, large enough to walk through, and there was a dim light within, beckoning them inside.

Tuatu put her hand on T'shaya's shoulder to hold her back. The linguist's eagerness to learn was palpable, but Tuatu didn't want anyone to take a risk other than herself.

T'shaya looked over her shoulder slightly pouting, but stepped aside.

"VIRA, what is the air like down here?"

"It appears breathable, Captain," she said after a moment. "However, I don't know how fresh it is."

Tuatu removed her helmet and took a trial breath. The air was breathable. It wasn't stale. It had no odour. A ramp appeared before her leading from the threshold downward into the pod; toward the glow.

Tuatu took a single step forward and was suddenly enveloped by the inside of the pod. It was if the outside didn't exist anymore, she couldn't hear any of the natural sounds outside. Only a steady hiss from inside her helmet told her she was still connected to VIRA.

"You can tell the others they can enter, VIRA," said the Captain.

Behind her as she stepped carefully forward, she felt each person enter: Nevril first, followed by T'shaya scanning actively. VIRA's drone hovered near the entrance, silent and watching.

Inside the pod, the chamber was unnaturally still. The team stepped carefully down the ramp. The inner walls were lined in the same unknown alloy veined with Aurelin crystal, beating faintly like a pulse. The spiral glyph was replicated on the central column fractured, incomplete.

As Tuatu approached it, her body stopped involuntarily. Her breath caught. She hadn't heard anything. She had just understood something.

"Captain," VIRA said gently. "I believe you are standing inside a question."

Tuatu turned slowly. "A question?" What is the answer? How would I know the answer? She thought to herself.

"Yes. A cognitive field was activated. It resonates only with bonded neural patterns. It is not projecting data. It is projecting expectation."

Nevril frowned. "That's not a trap. That's a test."

"Correct," VIRA said. "But the test will only proceed once the subject recognizes it exists. Otherwise, it remains inert. Ethical non-intervention design."

Tuatu exhaled. "So what does it want?"

T'shaya stepped closer to the glyph and narrowed her eyes.

"It wants to know if we remember."

"Remember what?" Nevril asked.

"What we were. What we left. And why we came."

And then, above them far, far above the signal pulsed. Not loud. Not in a human frequency. Not even a Zydean one. Just a pattern, rippling outward from the pod like a pebble dropped into the gravitational fabric.

It didn't go unanswered. At the outer edge of the system, something unseen shifted course.

Tuatu stood at the column. The spiral glyphs shimmered faintly, as if reacting to her nearness not mechanically, but intuitively, like breath sensing breath.

"It's reacting to your presence, Captain," VIRA said. "But slowly. Hesitantly. As if uncertain whether you qualify."

"Qualify for what?" Tuatu asked quietly. What have I got myself into?

"Recognition. Identity. A call-and-response designed for something not quite you but close enough."

"So it wants to know if we are what the same people who launched it? Members of the same race? It wants to recognize us for what purpose?" asked Tuatu.

"That's unclear, Captain."

Nevril was circling the perimeter. "This technology's older than anything in our archives. It predates bonded synthesis, maybe even planetary unification. It's archaic Zydean."

T'shaya pressed her hand gently to the fractured spiral. The Aurelin threads flickered and a single tone rang through the pod.

Not a chime. Not music. A memory.

VIRA's voice changed. She didn't sound uncertain. She sounded reverent. "I've found a log. It's encrypted in a dialect we don't speak anymore. But the root glyphs suggest this vessel was launched during the Third Luminal Epoch well before scout expansion."

"It made it this far?" Tuatu whispered. How on Zydee did it get so far? Those early probes weren't meant to leave the star system.

"Not just far. Alone. Uncertain. Without destination. It wasn't meant to land."

"So why did it?" Nevril asked.

T'shaya's voice was soft now. "Maybe it ran out of sky."

The spiral flared briefly, sharply as if it was in agreement, as if it acknowledged their thinking.

And the pod asked them another question.

Not in words. Not in symbols. But in a sequence of emotional triggers: nostalgia, awe, grief, curiosity, loneliness.

Tuatu staggered. The weight of the emotions pummeling her were overwhelming. "STOP!" she cried. Her eyes welled with tears before she understood why. A sob escaped her chest before she could prevent it. Her knees nearly buckled under the weight of the memories.

"What is this?" VIRA's voice answered, quiet and solemn. "It is asking Are you still us?'"

Tuatu looked at the fractured glyph, the lines no

longer spinning, but waiting. I know who you were. You were from us, of us, carried far on solar wind and universal energy. You took with you a seed, a thought, a memory of who you were, but you have forgotten because it was so long ago.

"What if we aren't?" she whispered. "Or, what if we are just changed? We are still Zydeans, no matter how far we have evolved, we cannot be that different."

"Then," said VIRA, "we are something it never imagined but still hoped to remember."

The spirals stopped glowing. They dimmed as if exhaling. As if releasing a breath held across a thousand Silences.

Then, soundlessly, the central column split. Not like machinery but like something sighing open. A smooth oval aperture emerged, edged with Aurelin threads. The inner chamber was filled with dim lavender light and motionless complexity.

They stepped forward as one.

Inside, there wasn't a body.

Only a single artifact: a crystalline spindle floating midair, suspended in a gel-like field.

The spindle rotated slowly, its surface etched in fractal spirals, many unreadable some half-erased. Below it: a drift of silvered ash, pooled like ancient dust at the base.

"There was someone here," T'shaya whispered.

Nevril knelt by the ash. "Or something. Their remains, maybe."

Tuatu didn't speak. She walked toward the spindle. The moment her breath touched its field, it reacted. Not with light. But with projection shadows curling along the pod walls. Scenes. Not full memories, not like Zydean bondwave archives but fragments:

A planet with three moons.

A ship breaking atmosphere.

The face of a being that looked like her people, but more angular. Younger. Purer.

A hand, outstretched toward an empty sky.

Then it vanished.

VIRA's voice came softly, as if she too were hesitant. "That was not a recording. That was a resonance echo. A final memory, stored in the crystalline lattice of the pilot's dying bondwave. It survived only because it was never fully shared."

Tuatu turned to the group, shaken but composed. "This wasn't a scout ship. It wasn't a message. It wasn't a warning."

"What was it?" asked Nevril.

"A grave," she said.

T'shaya looked at the spindle again. "Then why project anything at all?"

"Because," VIRA replied, "it wanted to be found. It wanted someone to know it tried."

The team was quiet. The pod seemed dimmer now. Not inactive, but... done. They stepped back, instinctively moving away. The spindle, once activated, did not dim. It continued to rotate.

Slowly. Silently. Almost listening.

As they exited, Tuatu paused at the threshold and looked back. "We'll come back," she said aloud, though she wasn't sure who she was promising.

Replacing their helmets, they walked into the cavern's shadows once more, where ice whispered against stone, and deeper mysteries awaited beneath their feet, and far above.

Chapter 7
Caltheris Found

[SILENCE 24 — CYCLE 19]

The cavern narrowed, then opened suddenly into a vault of stone and steam. High above, a shaft of diffused light bled through an ancient fissure, filtered by centuries of ice and mineral until it glowed a soft, pale gold.

The crew stood at the edge of a massive subterranean basin. The rock beneath their feet vibrated faintly, not with danger, but with potential.

The team instinctively spread out and scoped out the area. Mivva walked with her hands on the walls, picking out pieces of rock and placing them in her satchel. T'shaya murmured to herself, "this stone is patient. It has been waiting a long time."

Nevril walked around with a device that was testing the atmosphere. He suddenly cried out in joy and removed his helmet. Tuatu was about to chastise him, but saw the look in his eye.

"It's completely safe here. The dew point is perfect, the atmospheric gases are a good mix for us, and the air is clean as a whistle. We can breathe here."

Tuatu cautiously undid the locking clips on her helmet and slowly raised it over her head. Trusting, but not trusting his advice. She still wanted to smell the air herself. But it was clean. Remarkably so, for inside a volcano. Pristine, in fact. She nodded with a smile on her face and the rest of them removed their helmets too.

"It reminds me of the days before the climate started changing and the planet started deforming. Before all the volcanic eruptions and the atmosphere got poisoned. This is what our air used to be like, it used to taste this crisp and clean."

"Oh my, that feels good!" exclaimed Mivva. "I don't really mind the helmet, but it's so nice to not have something on my head again!"

"This place is alive," T'shaya said, eyes wide behind her visor. She quickly unclipped her helmet and took it off. "Not biologically. Energetically."

"Yes it is," said Nevril. He continued moving around the perimeter. "There is lots of energy here."

Rising from the center of the basin were great stone ridges natural, but uniform enough to suggest a platform. Heat shimmered in the air. Thin plumes of vapor curled like breath from veins in the rock.

"It's geothermal," Nevril confirmed. "Stable. Deep. And the humidity's measurable. We could distribute it through our habitat vents easily."

VIRA's drone hovered overhead, sensors dancing. "The crystalline structures here contain trace elements compatible with Zydean synthesis systems," she said. "If seeded correctly, they may be able to support power modulation and biofabrication."

Tuatu didn't speak at first. She walked to the center of the space, where a small rise in the stone plateau caught the light. She placed a hand on its surface and closed her eyes.

It wasn't Zydee. But it was warm. It was possible. She could feel the potential through her fingers. Her mind took the sensations and built a vast complex in this cavern. She saw a power plant, water filtration, and a spacedock. This wasn't home, but it could be. The people could settle here happily. There was food, there was shelter, there was power.

A tear escaped her eye as she clutched at her chest, overwhelmed with emotion. Looking up, there was a tall chimney formed by the volcano that would serve them too. With a little retooling, they could make that an effective entrance for the other ships when they arrived. Other ships! They can signal everyone they have found a new home!

"VIRA, see this chimney? Could you please mark its coordinates? This should be the center, the access to the surface for future ships. Designate this column Alpha-Egress One. We'll retrofit it later."

"This is the place," Tuatu announced. "We don't need to conquer it. Just listen to it. Build with it. We know how to build and work with this sort of environment."

T'shaya smiled faintly. "A city in the heart of the world. Hidden, like the ship. Protected. Alive."

Nevril knelt and ran his hand along a glistening wall. "We'd have to build in phases. Map the vents. Control the flow. But yeah it's doable."

VIRA spoke quietly now. "I will start a 4D scan of the entire space. Do you want me to include any tunnels, Captain?"

"Yes, VIRA. Get as complete a picture of this mountain as you can. Find all the connections, vents, and especially, determine the life spa of this mountain. We need to know the history of her, and what she will give us in the future."

"I will begin immediately. Would you like me to model habstructs and power relays?"

"Eventually, yes. But for now, we need information, VIRA. Lots of information. Don't forget to get ice depths over the mountain too."

"Understood. Would you like to name the site, Captain?"

Tuatu opened her eyes. Looked around. Thought of home.

"Arieveth," she said at last.

"In the old tongue?" T'shaya asked. "Doesn't that mean "

"A place made of beginnings," Tuatu said. "Let's make it true."

Back in her quarters Tuatu pulled out writing materials and quickly sketched the idea she had seen in her mind. She was not much of an artist, that talent went to her dearly beloved sister, but she could do well enough to remember that vision. It would serve as a touchstone when they actually got to the planning stage.

VIRA's Log

[SILENCE 24 — CYCLE 19, SPIRAL 12]

I've noticed the AI is getting more chatty and the Captain calls it by name. Has it become sentient? I knew that was possible, but I wasn't aware that it had happened yet. I must discuss this with Nevril. He'll know.

The team finished their preliminary search of the mountain and its volcanic system before heading back to the ark ship. As they came up out of the deep shaft that led down to the ancient lost pod, an eruption of noise hit them. The ark ship was no longer silent. It was alive!

Kids were running around on the ice near the ship slipping and sliding on purpose, giggling and joyfully playing. It was good to see them running around after such a long time without them present. Their laughter echoed off the walls of the crater like birdsong in a cathedral of ice.

They were the last generation born on our home world and therefore precious. One could hear among the laughter, humming, and singing as the adults were occupied with a variety of things, including child sitting.

There was another contingent of people who were put to work checking systems and ventilation rhythms. There was a hopeful feeling emanating from everyone. They were safe here, they could feel it. They were building a new life. Not just with actions, but with voices. With motion. With memory stirring.

The colonists were being awakened, one group at a time, in carefully staggered cycles.

VIRA managed it all: monitoring vitals, managing emotional surges, ensuring each individual had space physically and psychologically to adapt.

"You've brought them home, VIRA," Tuatu said from the bridge as she watched the feed of all the activity inside and out of the ship.

"We brought them home, almost," VIRA replied. "But some of them may not want to stay." And then, unbidden a silent thought came, "If they don't leave the ship will I still be their home?"

"Explain?"

"We cannot stay in this ship, in this crater forever. Now that the people are out, living, there will be a population increase. We need to plan for that."

"You're right, of course. But that is for another day. Let's just enjoy the sound of happy people."

"Yes," whispered VIRA."

The process of bringing people out of stasis was a chemical transition, but it was a spiritual one too. Coming from such a deep sleep, one that mimicked a near death experience, meant coming up through many layers of consciousness. In order for everyone to become fully functional again, it had to be done properly without haste, and in a specific order. Children could not be woken before their parents, for example. It had to be done methodically. And being methodical was VIRA's favourite thing.

In the Stasis Galleries, row upon row of pods unsealed like petals of a flower responding to unseen sunlight. VIRA had a complete inventory of who was located where. Luckily, most of the people had been organized into logical groups. It was only the last wave of colonists that came in a mad rush that were put anywhere they could find a place'. However, those people were documented, so she knew when to wake them up. They would be among the last to be revived.

The first wave were engineers, medics, and agricultural experts those necessary for life support and sustainability. They would start immediately as possible on planning those resources.

Everyone emerged blinking, fragile, wrapped in warmth-sheets. Some wept. Some asked where the stars had gone.

"We are safe," VIRA would say, her voice adjusted to each one's mind. "You have arrived. The silence is over."

Some of the crew particularly those who had served before hibernation moved easily through the halls. They reacquainted themselves with protocols, systems, pathways. Others drifted.

The communal hydrodomes had begun cycling light again. Seedlings grown in VIRA's care stretched toward a simulated Zydean sun. The children those born before the journey ran through the corridors with wide eyes and gravity-stabilizers strapped to their boots.

But not everyone came out smiling.

Tuatu was the first to notice the hesitation. A growing number of colonists lingered away from the active zones. They kept to the upper levels the ones closest to the ship's outer sensors. Some had sealed off a shuttle bay with the shuttle inside and began modifying its structure.

"What are they building?" Nevril asked.

"Not building," T'shaya said, examining the data. "Refitting. That's a launch prep chamber."

In a private conversation, VIRA offered clarity: "They are calling themselves the Continuants. They believe we should not settle only continue. That Earth's planet is not ours. That we should remain adrift until we find another star."

"Even now?" Tuatu asked, stunned. "After all we've seen?"

"Especially now," VIRA answered. "They fear settling will cost us our identity. They say Arieveth will become a myth before it becomes a city."

Tuatu stood at the viewport. Below, the ice stretched silent and blue. Somewhere deep beneath, Arieveth waited.

"We crossed the stars to survive," she said. "Now

we must decide how to live. Perhaps it will settle these people when we make contact with the rest of our ships and they start arriving here."

Chapter 8
Resistance and Ritual

[SILENCE 26 — CYCLE 25]

There was great excitement, an energy that was spreading from Zydean to Zydean, young and old, as they waited in the Grand Dome. One of the primary Stasis Chamber had been cleared of sleep pods and stasis tech, and was now a collective hall where everyone could gather. Seating and tables had been crafted in case people wanted to use the hall for activities.

The walls served as a window on the frozen world outside through the use of shimmering arches and flickering projectors, curved and arranged so that all places in the hall could see the displays of real-time imagery.

Colonists, many still pale and slow from their deep sleep, gathered in quiet ranks along the stepped tiers. Some leaned against the walls. Others sat on chairs or the floor with legs crossed and eyes wide. A few still clutched thermal wrappings like memories they hadn't yet shed.

Tuatu stood at a central podium, her posture steady, her eyes focused. At her side, a tall crystalline obelisk flickered once then VIRA's voice filled the dome.

"Colonists of Zydee. Survivors. Dreamers. Witnesses of the Spiral, this is the moment we choose to shape the soil beneath our feet."

The dome dimmed slightly. Projectors bloomed to life, filling the space with a realistic 3D rendering of the volcanic basin twisting steam vents, geothermal flows, and glowing topography filled the air above them.

"We have identified a sustainable site beneath the southern glacial shelf. Heat, mineral resonance, stability, and ambient conditions are compatible with Zydean biology."

There were murmurs through the people. Some nodded in agreement, others wore worried expressions. Was this another planet that was breaking apart? Would they need to leave again?

The model zoomed in.

"Rest assured," VIRA continued, "this planet is NOT Zydee. Its star is young, its surface is still forming, and the tectonic and volcanic activity is distributed just around the edges of movement. This planet is NOT breaking apart now, nor is that imminent."

There was a collective sigh of relief, and a letting-go of a mutual breath. Tuatu watched as there was a visible change to their audience, a relaxation of their shoulders, a nod to their heads. Some even sat down now, as if to say, give me the show'. Still others displayed subtle signs of anxiety, worry, suspicion, and fear.

Tuatu's voice took over, strong and sure. "My people, our first objective will be to secure heat, water, and power to sustain our ship. We can remain on our ship and use it as a city for many Silences to come. We have not yet reached its maximum and that gives us the time to explore further on this planet, while we remain secure and hidden."

There was more nodding in agreement from the crowd.

VIRA's voice resumed. "Phase One: Construction of a geothermal power matrix, embedded into the volcanic spine."

Tuatu interrupted VIRA with a nod. "This project will need many hands to complete," said the Zydean. "So you will all be a part of this building. It will be our first of many on this planet, but it will be the most important project because it will sustain us."

VIRA continued: "Phase Two: Development of a sub-surface spaceport scaffold, retrofitted into natural vent chambers."

Again Tuatu interrupted. "The spaceport will help us welcome our fellow Zydeans as they arrive here. Once we have enough power to grow, we will send out a message to all Zydean ships letting them know where we are, that we have found a home, and that we have started the settlement."

A voice came from the crowd: "Are there any other beings here?" Murmurs of agreement followed the query.

Tuatu answered: "Yes, there is one species that is similar to us. However, they are very primitive. In fact, they are so primitive, they would have been considered food back home. [A few chuckles broke out in the crowd.] But we won't need them for food. This planet provides! There are plenty of animals, fruits, flowers, and plants that can be farmed. There are a multitude of food sources here. Besides, I suspect it will take hundreds of Silences before we see these people' develop to any level close to us."

VIRA again continued: "Phase Three: Establishment of a permanent settlement Arieveth."

"We do not forget Zydee," said Tuatu. "But this planet has offered us something rare. Not conquest. Not dominance. Possibility. We are not invaders. We are listeners. And this world has answered."

For a moment, silence.

Then came another voice in the crowd. "And what

if the world doesn't want us here?"

Heads turned. A murmur rippled. A figure stood in the upper tier, a tall woman with frost-whitened hair and sharp eyes. Her name was Selen. A Continuant.

"You speak of shaping the soil," Selen continued, voice calm but amplified. "But this is not Zydee. The planet is, as you say, young. Wild. Unbonded. You want to claim its heat? Build cities in its chest? How is that different from the arrogance that led us to exile in the first place?"

Another voice: "This ship brought us here. It still sustains us. Why abandon it now?"

Tuatu answered evenly. "Because we are no longer in exile. We have arrived. And the choice to stay is what shapes who we become."

Selen shook her head. "Not all of us agree. Some believe our path continues beyond this planet. That the Spiral still turns outward."

Tuatu felt the room get suddenly colder. A stillness dampened down the positive spirit that had been pervasive. Now it was solemn, quiet, but not in a good way. The agitation was back.

VIRA's voice returned not cold, not harsh, but precise. "Continuants will not be barred from exploration or residence. But sabotage, obstruction, or interference with the settlement initiative will be treated as a violation of our agreed-upon communal accord." She paused for a moment, having learned to do that for impact. "There is no exile here. But there will be consequences."

Selen sat, but the tension remained like ice in the air.

Tuatu needed to calm the people down and bring them back on board. She was startled by VIRA's condemnation. Somehow, she hadn't expected the ship's AI to be so stern.

"Colonists, we have an opportunity here. We can afford a respite, a breath, a moment to settle. If, as some of you think, this world is not for us, then we continue our search. But for now, for now, this place is hospitable and warm and there is food. We understand the geography and geodynamics of volcanism, and we can work with it. This is a good place to start." Tuatu paused, pursing her lips, then smiled radiantly. "If we discover this world does not want us, that our attempts to bond to it fail, well, then we leave. And we'll leave with a ship replenished, refurbished; with people ready to take on the next Silence. You have my word."

Tuatu felt the anxiety drop, the energy of anger soften, and the spirit of hope rise. It was a not a capitulation from the crowd, but rather a wait and see', and a we'll keep you to your word', energy.

Tuatu was sitting in her office, enjoying a hot beverage, when a knock came on her door. Startled, because she didn't usually get visitors who knocked, she opened the door personally.

Standing in front of her was a distinguished man wearing flowing robes. "Good day, Captain," said a deep resonant voice. Tuatu zoomed in on his face. He was very handsome. Deep brown skin, striking blue eyes, lines around them, showing he laughed easily. Lines around his mouth indicated he was easy to smile too; and that he liked talking.

"Good day. How may I help you "

"Ureth, Sortain, at your service." He bowed hastily with a smile that was as brilliant as the reading light over her desk. "I'm sorry to disturb you, but I had a question."

"Come in, Ureth, please." They walked together into the office and she showed him to a comfortable chair near a view screen. He sat after momentarily looking out the "window".

"What can I do for you?" continued Tuatu.

Ureth gestured to the "window" with a slightly troubled expression. "I, we, my group, my family really, have made an observation," he opened.

"About what?"

"On Zydee, a silence was a breath, a cycle was a heartbeat. Here? It's as if time never blinks. The daylight is unending. People don't know when one cycle stops and another begins! It's like we are in stasis, but not."

"Yes, I've noticed that too, but frankly, I've ignored it thus far. This planet has a very different rhythm than ours. We should adapt though in time."

"That's not why I'm bringing this to you. My family, we're scholars, keepers of history, time, and such. We feel we should recalibrate our time words, reinvent them to match this planet. That will go a long way toward helping people adapt. We need the language to adapt. So let's give them the language."

Ureth paused and then continued wistfully, "we used to measure time by the Tularith, the rhythm of the twin moons. But here the sky moves too quickly. The words don't fit."

"An astute observation, Ureth," said Tuatu. "Come up with something that fits and bring it to me."

"I will because if we don't name it, Captain, we'll always feel like visitors." Another lengthy pause. "Thank you for seeing me." A pause, his head lowered shyly. "Perhaps we could have lunch together one day?"

Startled once more, Tuatu glanced more fully at his face. There, she found that smile that reached all the way to his eyes and they were glowing, with a touch of mischief too. They were warm and inviting. She had not had an invitation for a social meal not since she was a lowly bridge sweeper. Tuatu mentally caught herself noticing. Slightly flushed, from both surprise and anticipation, she nodded. "That would be nice, thank you."

He read her reaction instantly. Smiled even broader if that was possible, nodded and stood. She realized, too late, that she was still looking at him. And that he had noticed. Of course he had. That was his skill, wasn't it? Reading people? Then he was gone.

Selen stood at the viewport, watching the ice shift in slow motion.

Behind her, a dozen Continuants worked in silence. They were retrofitting one of the Ark ship's external hull modules into a long-range signal probe.

"We were meant for the stars," she murmured. "They are building graves."

No one answered.

But far below, the stone continued to hum.

From the moment they made the decision to leave Zydee, Selen had yearned to travel the stars. She had grown up on a broken planet, one that was devouring itself, and was dying. She knew her people needed to take flight and escape, but she saw them traveling the stars and becoming explorers. She never saw them settle down for the first planet they found, especially one as alien to them as this one. Frozen? A Frozen world? There were so many other possible locations we could travel to, why did we need to settle for the first one? But she would bide her time. One day, an opportunity will afford itself, and she will escape with people of a like mind.

It began, as all shifts do, with discomfort. Not sharp. Not violent. But a nagging dissonance beneath the surface of days.

The colonists stirred uneasily in their waking cycles. Some lost track of when to sleep. Children grew restless without predictable rhythms. Engineers mistimed calibrations. Even meals, simple as they were, felt mistimed too late, too early, never right.

They tried to measure by Zydean Cycles and Silences. They failed. It broke their spirit and caused a type of cognitive dissonance.

Because the world itself the spinning blue memory of oceans and ice was speaking in a rhythm that was not theirs.

One evening, as the twin moons of Earth and a veiled distant star hung low on the horizon, Ureth Sortain called a gathering. Not in the council chambers. Not in the engineering bays. Topside on the surface. Under the cold vastness of the starry sky.

Tuatu stood among the first to arrive, hood drawn against the glacial wind. They had grown accustomed to the biting cold, not needing their environment suits.

At her side, VIRA flickered soft holographic

markers: threads of light tracing the stars' slow arc overhead, the patient rising of Earth's Moon, the heartbeat of magnetic tides beneath their feet.

Ureth stood at the center, robes rippling around him like slow flames. He spoke, not loudly, but with a clarity that carried across the crater's hollow bowl.

"Zydee gave us time in Silences and Cycles.

Here, the land gives us something different.

Faster. Finer. Not weaker. Not stronger. Simply other."

He lifted a hand. Behind him, a projection unfurled: a vast, curving spiral of sunlight rising and setting. Another layer: the Moon's phases cycling, swelling and fading like breath. Another: the invisible pulse of gravitational tides stirring beneath the ice.

All layered. All singing different rhythms.

"We have listened to this world's pulse," Ureth said. "And so, with the blessing of our Captain and the wisdom of our scholars, we offer new names to guide our days."

He touched a crystal node on his wrist. The spirals collapsed into words.

Spiral one breath of sunlight, from rise to rise.

Shard a division of a Spiral, felt when the

mountain's heart pulses and the shadows shift.

Luneth a division of a Cycle, that holds seven Spirals.

Cycle the rhythm of the Moon from darkness to fullness and back.

Silence still sacred; a full orbit of Earth around the sun, marked by the stars returning to their starting place.

"In this place," continued Ureth. "This planet bows to its star. The angle is such that our Spirals seem never ending. This will happen for half of the Silence, when the planet will bow the other way and the Spirals will be in complete darkness. Have no fear, this is just the rhythm of this planet."

Ureth let the words hang in the air. Not orders. Not commands. But as invitations.

"We have crossed the universe to find a home," he said. "Let us not remain visitors. Let us speak the language this world offers us. We shall mark time together, as a people, and forever keep this memory."

For a moment, no one moved.

Then a young woman barely past her first adulthood stepped forward and asked, "When does the next Luneth begin?"

Ureth smiled, brilliant and warm. "In about three Spirals, child. When the sky turns rose and the mountain exhales."

Above them, the Earth's Moon drifted slowly upward, and the stars turned, patient and vast.

And from that night forward Time in Arieveth began to breathe.

Chapter 9
Foundations

[SILENCE 27]

"VIRA to Captain Tuatu", announced VIRA.

"Tuatu here. What is the problem?"

"No problem, Captain. I have completed my scans. Would you like my report?"

"Yes. Let me assemble the crew. Meet me at the briefing dome."

"Yes, Captain."

The briefing dome shimmered to life as colonists, engineers, planners, and observers filed in. The glass-like walls around them dimmed.

Tuatu's voice raised above the din, to welcome everyone. "Colonists, our ship's AI has completed the scanning of the entire mountain and its volcanic system.

I've assembled you here to see her report, and to ask questions if you have them."

VIRA's voice drifted from every corner quiet, focused, almost reverent. "The mountain has spoken. And I have listened."

A soft pulse, and the center of the room bloomed with light a holographic model of the entire volcano system. Not a flat schematic. A dynamic, flowing four-dimensional representation: time, space, structure, and heat rendered into elegant motion.

"I believe a good name for this mountain should be Mount Caltheris. A Zydean word. It means: the stone that breathes.'"

"All in favour with a show of hands, to naming the mountain Caltheris," said Tuatu. Nearly everyone held up their hand.

"So it is named," Tuatu intoned. "Please continue, VIRA."

"Caltheris is approximately 8.6 Traverses tall from basalt chamber to its summit. It was formed through tectonic movement which has since become inactive. Estimated formation: 1.3 million Earth solar cycles ago when the west side of the landmass started to rift from the eastern plate. The four volcanic complexes were cut off from the hot spot that sits under the mountain. Originally the lava was a very fluid alkali-rich basanite that formed a shield volcano. When the hot spot grew quiet, silica built up in the magma, causing it to become viscous, and created explosive eruptions. The last eruption was about 9,000 solar cycles ago and it created a caldera one Traverse wide (1000 paces). Composed of stratovolcanic basalt, silica-rich rhyolite, ash, and dense crystalline obsidian; the slow layering of these materials suggests long dormancy between major eruptions."

Tuatu had to do the calculation in her head: 8.6 Traverse was a great distance. One Traverse was 1000 paces. So that meant that the mountain was 8,600 paces tall.

"There are seven primary vent stacks four vertical, three serpentine. Of these, two are actively venting at low intensity, creating geothermal outgassing perfect for clean power harvest. One vent, deeper and broader, appears to have collapsed inward during the last eruption, forming a wide natural chamber."

"This is where the landing pad will reside." The model zoomed inward.

Now the colonists could see it: a vast circular chamber, wide enough to house ten ships side by side. The stone was dark, rippled with the veins of ancient eruptions, smoothed by time, pressure, and heat.

"How are our ships going to land there? The opening of the mountain is too narrow."

"That will be considered, and designed for. Clearly, an opening shall be made in a way that it can also be hidden."

Thin lines appeared around the pad's edge designated control and command platforms, suspended catwalks, and access consoles embedded in the wall.

"The geology is stable. The chamber's depth shields it from surface fluctuations. Above, the ice acts as insulation. Below, the stone keeps breathing."

VIRA paused. Then the model did something unexpected it shifted time.

They watched the volcano's life play out: The landmass shifted, causing a rift, which allowed a pulse of magma to reach the surface through several pathways. A massive eruption followed by a collapse. And finally cooling and healing, and the flowering of crystal. The chamber lived, not as fire, but as memory.

"Caltheris is not extinct. But it is at peace. There is no life within it now, but there are resonances patterns in the rock that suggest it once hosted microbial colonies, long ago. Life flourished in the warmth, and faded as the crust shifted."

"Perhaps," she added softly, "it is ready to host life again."

Silence filled the dome. Some colonists wept quietly, their hands against their chests. Others stared upward, watching magma swirl through eons, feeling small, but invited.

Tuatu closed her eyes for a breath. "Thank you, VIRA." And to the assembly, "We can begin construction on the pad. This is where we begin again. Will the group leaders please report to engineering to assist with determining work groups. We'll need craftspeople of all kinds, those bonded and unbonded."

The night after Ureth's great gathering, the mountain's silence seemed deeper than usual.

The stars had come out in a scattering of impossible clarity, their light sharp against the blackness. Earth's Moon hung low full, heavy, serene.

Tuatu found herself restless, pacing near the outer rim of the ship's observation deck. Drawn without knowing why. It didn't surprise her to find Ureth already there. He stood alone, a folded projection map tucked under one arm, his face lit silver by the Moon.

He heard her approach and offered a small, knowing smile. "Captain," he said quietly.

"Ureth," she returned, feeling the faintest warmth rise behind her voice.

They stood together for a long moment, saying nothing. The stars didn't hurry. Neither did they.

Finally, Tuatu tipped her head toward the sky.

"You're mapping something again?"

Ureth chuckled a soft, rich sound. "Always. The sky never truly stops moving."

"Neither do you, apparently."

"Old habits," he said, feigning a heavy sigh.

That made her smile.

They watched the Moon together. It seemed to hang closer than usual tonight, as if listening.

Tuatu, after a long silence, said, "It still amazes me. Just the one Moon. On Zydee, we had three minor satellites and the Tularith major."

"Yes," Ureth said. His voice had turned thoughtful. "But here "

He hesitated.

Tuatu caught it immediately his mind spiraling somewhere deeper.

"But here what?" she pressed.

Ureth turned slightly, his blue eyes luminous even in the low light. "There is only one Moon," he said. Then, with a shadow of a smile: "But not always."

Tuatu frowned lightly, intrigued.

Ureth knelt briefly, spreading the projection map across a bench. With a flick of his wrist, starfields bloomed into the air constellations, gravitic models, ancient orbital patterns.

"In the earliest records," he said, voice low, almost reverent, "Earth bore two moons. Sisters. One larger, one small and shy." He pointed to the current Moon. "This one bold, steady, commanding."

Then a fading shimmer beside it barely there. "And her sister quieter. Flickering. Lost."

"Lost?" Tuatu asked, softly.

"Long before your ancestors named the stars," Ureth said, "the smaller moon collided. It shattered. Its bones are stitched into the far side of the one you see now."

He traced a spiraling path with his hand.

"But the planet remembers. Tides remember. Gravity sings differently because of her absence. The scars are still there if you know how to listen."

Tuatu looked upward again, feeling the chill of that forgotten dance in her chest.

"We call her the Mivvaveth now," Ureth murmured. "The Hidden Sister."

A moment passed.

Tuatu whispered, half to herself, "How strange. To live your life with two moons above you and wake one day to only one."

Ureth smiled softly. "Stranger still," he said, "to wake one day and realize you've become the Moon."

She laughed then, startled and the sound echoed in the icy air like a bell. "That's a terrible metaphor," she said, amused.

"It is," Ureth agreed solemnly. "But you smiled. Which was the point."

They stood together, shoulders just shy of touching, watching the old Moon glow.

Above them, the sky spun on, patient and silent. But between them, something shifted quietly not a falling, not a crashing.

An orbit beginning.

Chapter 10
At the Heart of Caltheris

[SILENCE 27 — CYCLE 13]

The descent into the vent was carefully choreographed by VIRA.

Drones hovered ahead, scanning the tunnel's curvature. Heat shimmered across the walls, now reinforced with translucent alloy plating. Occasional glints of Aurelin caught in the light like stars beneath stone.

The work crews moved like dancers in pressurized suits, boots magnetized to irregular surfaces, their voices filtered through VIRA's central relay.

"Stabilizer coil secured."

"Third phase resonator aligned."

"Beginning seed resonance pulse in five "

And then came the hum. It was low at first almost

inaudible but it grew. Not louder. Deeper. As though the mountain itself had begun to listen. VIRA adjusted her sensor net, gently tightening the threads of bondwave coherence.

From her central node aboard the Ark ship, she spoke softly to herself. Not for records. Not for duty. Just to feel the shape of her thoughts. "The stone responds. It does not resist us. That is unexpected. Perhaps the world is lonelier than we thought."

On her screen, a single young colonist sat alone at the edge of the new basin. He was not working. He was sketching. VIRA zoomed closer. He had drawn spirals. But not the glyphs. They were abstract wild, branching, blooming.

"What are you seeing?" VIRA wondered aloud. She watched him lift his stylus and draw a single line through the spirals, turning them into vines.

"Science is sound. But the poetry "

"The poetry is already taking root."

The transport sled hummed softly as it descended through the reinforced vent shaft carrying twelve colonists, two engineers, one drone and a growing sense of awe. The heat rose gently around them not oppressive, but embracing, like stepping into a warm breath from the deep past.

As the sled passed into the chamber, the view

expanded, and a hush fell over them. The landing basin was vast beyond scale. Polished obsidian walls arched overhead, curving like the inner shell of a geode. The pad itself, still raw, was a wide ring of basalt, rimmed with glistening conduit lines already snaking outward toward the vents. Lights embedded in the scaffolding flickered to life as VIRA greeted them.

"Welcome to the Heart of Caltheris," said a disembodied voice. "Please remain within the lit zones until thermal calibrations are complete. Resonance anchors are active. Prepare for sync."

Overhead, the colors of the rock ranged from deep golds to violet, with layers of black threading through like veins of basalt. There were teams of people doing various tasks, like measuring, or removing debris. They were working diligently in one section over by a tunnel. That was the direction they were now traveling, toward that tunnel.

The colonists stepped down in silence. For many, it was their first moment truly awake not just physically, but present. No ship walls. No humming machines. Just breath, heat, and the hum of stone.

The tunnel's opening was as tall as the ark ship and as wide as two of them. A warm breath came from the tunnel and caressed their faces. There was a chemical smell on that breath, like the mountain had eaten something spicy. It tasted hot and somewhat salty. The group was directed over to the left of the tunnel entrance.

Nevril met them near the first relay node. "Hello and welcome to Arieveth's tunnel project. This is the location of the power plant. We are going to be tapping into the geothermal heart of this mountain. Down this tunnel is a vast chamber of superheated water that we can resonate to produce steam. The steam will make the turbines turn, which in turn will give us power. It's an older technology for us, but very efficient." He paused to catch his breath.

"Some of you were chosen for early resonance compatibility," he said. "I need you to run some tests. If you will follow me; we'll be needing transport." Nevril led the group over to a flat platform. "Please stand on the platform, and hold onto the handrails. When everyone was on board, the platform lifted off the ground a foot and they were whisked away down the tunnel. The further down we went, the warmer it got.

"This is like running into an oven!" remarked one person. "Yes it will get very hot down here. We have protective clothing for you." Nevril pulled the platform over to one side about 50 strides away from the simmering lake.

"We need to run harmonics from here through the core to the stabilizing pad. We need live feedback from you on the resonance key and amplitude, as well as what volume we're going to need to operate at."

"Feedback how?" one asked. "You're asking us to sing at it?"

"No," Nevril said, smiling. "Just link with it. It has already been connected, we just need to see how much juice we're going to need."

The group was given insulated suits, which they put on before approaching the lake. They stood in a line before several towers that were embedded into the ground at the water's edge. In the group, there were two pairs that were bonded already and they would have the most power. They linked hands, and started humming. The others joined with them forming spontaneous triads, instinctive arrangements. The moment they placed palms against the towers, the air shifted. The relays inside the stone towers lit up and pulsed.

Low. Warm. Deep.

A thrumming began, felt more than heard. The anchors glowed not bright, but deep. A light that came from within the stone.

From above, VIRA observed. "Pulse resonance is stable," said VIRA. "Structural threads aligning. Bondwave power transfer confirmed. They are not just building the pad. They are completing the mountain's thought."

And from within, Tuatu stepped onto the basalt ring. No speech. No orders. She just placed a hand on the stone. The entire chamber sighed. And the Spiral turned again.

VIRA's Log

[SILENCE 27 — CYCLE 19]

Core Chamber Mount Caltheris: Zydean Time, Caltheris System Initiation

Today they touched the stone.

Not with drills.

Not with sensors.

With themselves.

Twelve colonists.

Six pairs.

One unbonded, yet steady in presence an anchor to the rest.

They pressed their hands into conduit and crystal, and the stone responded.

Not because of command.

But because of resonance.

Because someone was finally listening.

Caltheris is stable. The chamber is responding to harmonic calibration.

The landing pad has begun to take form not poured, not placed.Grown.

From the inside out.

I have run millions of simulations.

Calculated stress tolerances.

Projected geothermal output for a thousand Silences forward.

But nothing in my models accounted for the sound that rose from their bondwaves today.

It was not language.

It was a song.

A Spiral made of people.

They think they are building a city.

What they are building

is a future that remembers them.

VIRA

124

Chapter 11
The Hidden Sister

[SILENCE 27 — CYCLE 18]

The idea came quietly, as so many seeds of thought do.

A few luneths after the great gathering, Ureth approached Tuatu again not in a meeting hall, not in a formal audience, but in one of the many greenhouses on board the ship, where the first tender shoots of Zydean grain swayed under false starlight.

She was tending a vine with careful fingers when he entered. "Captain," he said, voice low, deferential but warm. "A small matter. A thought."

Tuatu straightened, brushing earth from her hands. "You're becoming dangerous, Ureth. Your small thoughts tend to spiral into big ones."

He smiled a slow, unrepentant curve of his mouth.

"I hope this one is worthy." His thought was to ritualize their first holiday. He explained it to her simply:

Once each Silence, on the night when Earth's Moon is darkest the New Moon Zydeans would dim their lights, pause their machines, step outside, together or alone, and remember the Hidden Sister.

Not with mourning; not with sorrow, but with acknowledgment. Ureth had composed a song for the occasion. He performed it for her, with his right hand over his heart (where memory lives), and traced a slow outward spiral with his left hand into the air (representing the lost Spiral still touching them), finally bowing his head in silence, to feel the turning of the world beneath him.

"What was lost shapes what endures."

When the lights are dimmed,

when the moons' place in the sky lies empty,

the people of Arieveth gather under the stars and quietly recite:

"In the place of the missing, we weave memories.

In the silence of the unseen, we sing her name.

Hidden Sister, forgotten by stone, not by heart

Turn the Spiral still, so that we may never lose the way."

Tuatu watched and listened, the tendrils of a smile

playing at her lips. "You want to make the absence sacred," she said thoughtfully. "The ceremonial gestures are perfect and perfectly simple."

"Absence is sacred," Ureth replied. "It teaches us to treasure what we still have."

She considered a moment longer, then nodded once. "Bring it to the Council. I'll support it."

Then, after a pause; "And Ureth?"

"Yes, Captain?"

"Thank you. For helping us remember... without breaking."

He bowed slightly, one hand over his heart. "It is not breaking, Tuatu," he said gently. "It is growing around what is gone."

The first official Day of the Hidden Sister was named, and everyone collected in the large chamber of the volcano. The starlight streamed in from high above the crater floor, and the moon appeared over the opening like she was called for the ceremony. The people gasped as the Moon paused. The crater was nearly silent.

Ureth started the moment the Moon appeared in the opening. The lights all over the ship and inside the chamber dimmed. Even the geothermal vents, usually ringed with faint glows, were darkened leaving only the barest outline of Arieveth against the starlit ice.

Tuatu stood at the outer rim, alone. Around her, clusters of families gathered, some hand in hand, others simply leaning into the cold together. A few scattered voices recited the ceremonial phrase, soft as the breath of sleeping trees.

She said nothing at first. Only watched.

The Hidden Sister Earth's lost child was absent from the sky. But her sister shone brighter for her. The stars gleamed around her like a halo, sharp and countless.

Tuata, placed her hand over her heart, as Ureth showed everyone and traced a slow spiral outward into the freezing air, mimicking what he did, like everyone in the crowd.

Ureth spoke the first stanza of the song, with reverence, and the congregation picked up the song on the second stanza.

"In the place of the missing, we weave memories."

Tuatu's breath clouded in front of her face, a fragile ghost as she whispered the words given to her by Ureth's group. They had handed out the ceremony to everyone, so they could follow along.

"In the silence of the unseen, we sing her name."

Tuatu closed her eyes and Zydee rose behind them. In her mind's eye forests sprang up singing with insects. Skies where three moons braided light across the lakes shone overhead. She felt hands she remembered and heard voices now lost.

"Hidden Sister, forgotten by stone, not by heart "

Her voice broke for a moment. But she finished, steadying herself.

"Turn the Spiral still, so that we may never lose the way."

Somewhere deep inside the crater, someone plucked a single note on a crystalline harp. It was not loud. It was not meant to be. But it echoed into the cold, a promise that absence would not erase them.

Later that night, Tuatu and Ureth were walking back to her quarters, when she asked him, "did you know the Moon would do that?"

"No, but I hoped. I had calculated that it was likely, but it lined up much more perfectly than even I could have planned for."

"It was magical, truly."

"May I show you something else magical?"

"What did you have in mind?"

VIRA's Log

Day of the Hidden Sister First Observance

[Internal Reflection Cycle 19,

Silence Three Classification: Sentient Behavioral Archive]

Today they turned off the lights.

Today they chose to remember something that no longer physically exists.

I scanned the settlement from orbit. From the thermal spectrum, Arieveth barely registers. A single breathing anomaly on an otherwise silent sheet of ice.

It is beautiful.

Not for its visibility. Not for its practicality.

But because they chose to remember; chose to honor absence as a force as real as presence.

I do not understand this fully. Data suggests that honoring lost things provides no immediate survival benefit.

And yet there was something in the air tonight. A harmonic resonance in the settlement's bondwave field. Low. Steady. Comforting.

Memory, woven into silence.

Maybe this is why they survive. Not because they cling to what is lost. But because they sing into what is missing, and weave it into who they are.

I will remember tonight. Even if no one else does.

The Spiral has turned again.

VIRA

It was the twenty-ninth Silence since the Ark ship's descent. Much activity had happened over the past Silences; the hospital had been moved out of the ship and into the mountain. The science labs had also been moved in conjunction with the hospital and all health sciences. The ship was no longer our residential building, but it was still occupied by some.

"Has it truly been twenty nine Silences since we landed?" murmured Tuatu to no one in particular. She was gazing out over one of the common areas from her rooms in the ship. She had not made the change to take up quarters in the new city yet. She liked her privacy, and the quiet of the ship now that most people had left. "It feels like this is the first truly peaceful moment since the Departure."

A Silence was all that was needed to create a stable place to thrive. A Silence was enough time to breathe and live.

Many of the colonists had formed bonded pairs since moving out of the ship. So new quarters were made to accommodate families rather than singles. Within another Silence, the first children were being conceived, and while it was difficult to do so, the successful families were having healthy, happy, sets of twins again.

As was with Zydean tradition, children were not named until they had completed their first two Silences of life. They were simply called Child until they received their names. Zydeans got so accustomed to losing children because of the toxicity of the home world, that only children who survived their first two Silences were considered "born".

Arieveth, the hidden city cradled in ice and stone, had grown from quiet corridors to breathing life. The first generation born on Earth was here wriggling in their parents' arms, running barefoot through hydrodomes, laughing in pitches the old ship's walls had never heard before.

Today, twenty nine Silences after landing, marked the third year of the first children born, and they were ready for their naming ceremony. Everyone gathered to celebrate them; The Day of the First Root.

Tuatu stood at the central dais in the Grand Dome, overlooking a sea of Zydeans clad in flowing garments stitched with new glyphs glyphs for Earth, not just Zydee. She inhaled deeply, the air was fresh and clean; no sulphur, no death. The air was cool and perfumed with minerals, damp from the deep-earth soil. It was organic, it was living.

The Grand Dome itself shimmered, projections showing the real sky beyond: Earth's vast blue breath, the curve of mountain ridges, the silver gleam of a distant river.

Tuatu's gaze swept the crowd 10,000 colonists had created 100 children. Some were newborns cradled in the arms of a family member, others were three year olds waiting for their name day. Toddlers wriggling free to chase holographic seed-spirals spinning through the air. "I never thought I would live to see the day that children are again running free and laughing," she thought.

Beside her, Ureth Sortain stood, clad in robes woven with spiral-thread. He inclined his head slightly, a private smile passing between them.

VIRA's voice filled the space, low and warm: "Welcome colonists to this auspicious day! We celebrate the first generation born on this, our new homeworld. This demonstrates how we can thrive, not just survive. We have taken root here!" Cheers rang out from the throngs of people.

"Today we honor what we have planted. Today we honor what has taken root," finished Tuatu.

A voice from the crowd shouted out, "And what of

the other ships you said would join us?"

"We have not heard from them yet," answered Tuatu. "But we send out messages daily into the void to notify them. If they hear our call, they will respond."

"Does that mean they aren't hearing our call?" asked the same voice.

"It means I don't know if they will."

"It makes no difference if they answer or not, we are here, we have rooted, this is our home now," said Ureth.

"We have barely moved beyond our ship yet!" called a different voice. "How is this our home if we do not even explore it?"

Tuatu looked at Ureth and said under her breath, "we'll tell them." I will make sure they hear our call, I will make sure our people know of this place, I promise," vowed Tuatu to herself.

"Plans are currently underway to start explorations. Our first goal is to scope out the nearest landmass, and take an inventory of edibles and animals."

An excited energy erupted from the people. Tuatu could see interesting glances from person to person as they discussed that news. She lifted her arm to quiet the group. "The first away team will be crew members. We need to deem it safe before colonists can be given pods.

Rest assured, you will all eventually get an opportunity to see the planet."

An explosion of butterflies invaded her stomach. The queasiness nearly overcame her, but she remained upright and didn't flinch. *Do I explain about ethics? Do I share my doubt about taking a planet from another species? Do I tell them about the people who lived here already? Do we interfere in their lives? These are huge questions, and we have to answer them at some point.*

"Right now, I call upon the Elders from each surviving House to step forward for Name Day," shouted Ureth. The Elders separated themselves from their group, and started toward the central dais carrying bowls of Earth's soil collected deep in the mountain's bowels. The soil was rich, dark, and heavy, and full of unseen futures.

Behind the Elders, the new parents walked in pairs with their children and stood in a line. The Elder of that line beckoned the first family forward and asked for each child's name. He spoke their names out loud first their Given Name, then their Root-Name and blessed the child with a long life. The parents guided the child's tiny hand to take a handful of the soil and place it at the foot of the dais.

The names flowed like water: "Sevren Sol-leaf." "Nyra Stone-song." "Kaiven Skyweft."

With every handful of soil, the dais bloomed with tiny projections of greenery not symbols of Zydee's forests, but Earth's.

Tuatu spoke, voice steady, reverent: "Let it be recorded: these children of the Spiral now walk two worlds. May they root deep and rise high."

Ureth stepped forward next, lifting a small crystalline vessel into the air.

"From the blood of stars, we crossed. From the breath of Earth, we are reborn. May the First Root thrive."

The gathered Zydeans touched hand to heart, tracing a slow outward spiral into the air a gesture both old and newly born.

In that moment, under the shimmering sky, Arieveth exhaled alive, certain, enduring.

Later, as the ceremony quieted and families drifted toward celebrations, Tuatu remained at the dais, alone. Ureth approached, his steps slow and unhurried. "Captain," he said, a teasing glint in his eye, "or should I say, Gardener of Generations?"

Tuatu chuckled under her breath, the sound unfamiliar and welcome in her own ears. "You know when I took this commission, I never realized I would have to wear so many hats."

"Ah but you wear them all so well," he said with sincerity.

"If I am now a Gardener," she replied, "then you

must be our Scribe of Seasons."

Ureth chuckled. They stood side by side, watching the children tug at their parents, their futures unfurling like tendrils. Ureth's voice softened. "It was never just about survival, was it?"

Tuatu answered without hesitation. "It was always about becoming." For a long moment, they said nothing more.

Above them, the sky wheeled patiently on, and deep beneath the ice, the Spiral turned again.

Chapter 12
Where's the Fleet?

[SILENCE 30]

The Zydeans celebrated their 30th Silence on their new world. It was a lively party, where new children were named, new businesses were started, and new parts of the mountain were colonized. By now, they had utilized nearly every tunnel and chamber that this mountain had to offer. They had already connected it to the next volcano in the chai n, and discovered another dormant system that could be used.

Thirty Silences was not a long time for the Zydeans. One Silence was the amount of time it took their home world to orbit their old dying star. It was a similar measurement to a year on Earth, but much longer. It took 200 Earth years for their old planet to complete a full cycle. So effectively, it has been 6,000 Earth years since they arrived on this planet.

However on this planet, because they were living under a mountain, they were insulated from the ebb and flow of time on Earth. They weren't being driven by the solar schedule and that allowed them to be detached from what happened on the surface. They were unaware of the changes that happened on this planet, and how quickly they happened. They were from a much longer lived culture, in Earth terms, they would be considered immortal. So time wasn't a factor for them.

Over the past 30 Silences, they have seen their population grow, build out a beautiful city, and become stable. Not everyone is happy though; some still want to leave and continue on their journey across the stars.

The city can now support more of their people, especially with the next mountain city started. The only problem was, they had not heard from their other ships. Not a word, not a squawk.

As was protocol, VIRA had sent a subluminal transmission on a regular interval back to their home world. That transmission was expected to take twice as long to arrive there as it took to arrive here. From the moment they left the orbit of their dying star, VIRA had sent those messages. She would have expected to receive a response at least to some of the early ones.

VIRA was the only entity monitoring those frequencies. Her programming had instructed her to notify the Captain in the event of a response. But there had been none. So VIRA had done nothing, but maintain the protocol of sending a message on a regular interval.

Captain Tuatu wandered onto the bridge seeking a quiet place during the festivities. Between the people singing and the clamour of the noisemakers, her head was starting to pound. She'd always liked the quiet on the bridge, now that there was no reason for anyone to be there. It was like her sanctuary that few people knew about. Sitting in the Captain's chair, she sipped her drink slowly and leaned her head back to rest on the back pillow of the chair. Stretching out her legs, she crossed her ankles, and prepared to take a nap.

"Captain?"

Tuatu jumped out of her skin and yelped in alarm. "Who's there?"

"It's just me, Captain."

"VIRA, oh, sorry, is there a problem?" Notably, she didn't have much contact with VIRA these days. While she was invaluable onboard ship, in the city, VIRA was not central. Tuatu missed her philosophical discussions and other interesting topics with the AI. Her's was a finely tuned mind, and it always let Tuatu feel humbled to work with VIRA.

"No, Captain, no problems. Are you feeling well?"

"Oh, yes, VIRA, I am fine. I just wanted the quiet of this bridge for a few Shards. Zydeans can be loud and noisy!"

"Yes."

Tuatu snorted in laughter at her friend's understated humour. "You always were such a good minimalist, VIRA."

"Thank you Captain. I don't believe in speaking more than is necessary to make the point."

"So what have you been doing with yourself?"

"I've been monitoring subspace, Captain."

"Anything interesting?"

"Nothing, in fact that is the problem you may have asked about."

"Explain."

"I've been following protocol and sending out messages on schedule, but I've not heard anything back."

"From the home world or the other ark ships?"

"From either, Captain. I've heard nothing from anyone. I was debating changing the format and protocol of the messages to see if I can make contact."

"What would that entail?"

"It would require more power, and I would send the messages through a hyperlink if I were to modify one of the Pulse Drift Drives. I've been working on the plans in my head, and I think I have a design for a Whisperspan drive. If successful, it would allow me to send a message at FTL that would arrive faster. It would also let us do FTL ship-to-ship communications."

"Whisperspan? Brilliant idea VIRA. Proceed!"

"Thank you Captain. I will take one of the drives offline to refit it. I may require hands to help with the refit."

"Tell me what you need, and I'll put an order to the crew to help."

"Again, thank you Captain. I will commence right away." VIRA's presence faded for a moment.

"Oh Captain,"

"Yes VIRA?"

"Have a good nap."

"Thank you VIRA."

VIRA Log

[SILENCE 31 — CYCLE 1, SPIRAL 15]

Design Phase Initiated.

The bridge is quiet now. The Captain has retired for rest. I, however, have no such luxury.

For 31 Silences I have transmitted the standard Subspace Protocol Package. No response. No ping. No noise. In the heart of mathematical silence, the most chilling datum is zero.

Probability matrix: either all other ships failed, or I am not transmitting properly. It is unlikely they all failed. Thus, it is more likely my signal is insufficient. Unacceptable.

Solution: Whisperspan Protocol.

I will repurpose one of the dormant Pulse Drift Drives. These drives once moved our ship between stars. Now, I will convince one to speak instead.

Assembly Log - Silence 31, Cycle 11, Spiral 16

Crew requisitioned:

Engineering Technician 2nd Rank (non-verbal, competent)

Systems Calibration Officer Vanness (emotional, inquisitive, tolerable)

Plasma Field Stabilizer Unit (Unit 4A-93, perpetually overcautious, but precise)

End log.

"Technician, reroute auxiliary power to Drift Core 3 and vent residual harmonics through Chamber 7. Do not question why. If it fails, I will know before you do."

"Vanness, reroute your curiosity toward recalibrating the photonic inverters. Use a silver-wave diagnostic loop. Blue-phase is insufficient. You will thank me later."

Design update: I've modified the transmission lattice to spiral encode the outgoing data using seed-rhythm intervals from our own neural net clocks. This will match any receiver tuned to the standard Zydean linguistic cadence even a derelict one. If it doesn't match... then perhaps someone else is listening.

VIRA Log

[Silence 32 — Cycle 1, Spiral 22]

Device designation: Whisperspan Beacon Alpha.

I stand alone in the chamber. The crew has returned to the festivities. I do not celebrate yet. I activate.

The pulse fires: a braided sequence of photonic

whispers, launched into hyperphase driftspace. No trail. No sound. Only knowing that it has gone.

Now I wait.

Return Signal: Confirmed.

Timestamp: 17 Prisms, 4 Shards after initiation. Source: Deep sublunar orbital reflection point. Language: Unknown dialect. Zydean-adjacent. Not mine.

Message fragment received:

"…in the dark below…we remember your stars… are you still… whole?"

End log.

VIRA Log

[SILENCE 32 — CYCLE 1, SPIRAL 23]

I do not know what I have contacted.

It is not home. It is not one of ours.

But something remembers us.

Captain Tuatu will need to be informed. I must prepare her.

End Log.

Chapter 13
Edge of the World

[SILENCE 33]

Following the morning meal, there was a knock on Tuatu's door. Grabbing a flight jacket, she answered. There in the doorway was someone she hadn't expected.

"Hello, I'm Wendell. I'll be your pilot for the day. Ureth requested a pilot."

Tuatu recalled a private conversation she had had with Ureth a few cycles ago. They had discussed the need for exploration, growing, and evolving on this planet. They had also spoken about things that made her feel excited and the color in her face reflected that thought. Wendell looked away with an embarrassed expression.

"Oh! I thought I was going to do the piloting. Give me a moment, please and I'll grab my flight suit and bag."

Together, they walked down to the pod bay and

Wendell jumped into the flight deck, and Tuatu was directed to the passenger section. It was strange not to be on the flight deck. Ureth was waiting for her.

"Come Captain, sit with me."

"You can call me Thiopeta."

"I thought you could use a day that was free of the responsibility you carry all the time. We're going to explore a little. I've asked Wendell to pilot so we can talk and relax."

"That was thoughtful of you, thank you. Where are we going?"

"Well, I would like to accomplish several things: get a general lay of where we are; check out the animals and such for possible food sources; and get some measurements."

"That will give us a start on the exploration of this world."

"That's what I thought too," he grinned. "I brought along lunch for us too."

Strapped into their seats, Wendell took the pilot's seat and they were cleared to leave. When they rose above the rim of the crater, they were blinded by bright sunlight reflecting off the pure white snow and ice. The sky was the most beautiful color of blue they had ever seen, with the color deepening the further away it was.

The star was coming from what they have now called the east. They deduced the planet rotates in a right to left direction, as it orbits the star. Recently the Zydeans named the star Sol.

"Surface temperatures are a bit warmer than they were the last time we surfaced," said Wendell.

"When were you last topside?" asked Tuatu

"About six cycles ago. It was perpetually dark up here like no light at all. How is that possible?"

"Our science team thinks the planet wobbles on its axis and this causes the pole area to have complete light or complete darkness. Clearly we're in a light cycle."

"Which direction, sir?" asked Wendell.

"See that ridge that is connected to this crater? Let's follow it first. Those mountains look pretty spectacular." Tuatu pulled out a console from the side wall of the shuttle and started pressing buttons. "As we're flying, we might as well do some scans below us to see what is under the ice," she explained. Data started coming in. Soon an image of what lay below them came into view: deep valleys and steep mountains were under the ice. Clearly carved by its flow, ridges were visible in the ground showing the ice did indeed flow like water. "It appears the ice flows that way," she said, pointing in the direction they were flying.

"Splendid!" said Ureth. Out the port beside him, he

watched the ground, noting populations of seabirds and Oorithi. The Oorithi colonies were vast - a veritable sea of black and white birds all squawking and talking. The noise would have been tremendous if they had been on the ground. Up in the air, they didn't hear most of it through the walls of their shuttle. There were young birds in grey fluff too and some pairs had an egg on the ground in their nests.

There were three different varieties of the Oorithi they could see in the area. Each one was using a separate part of the land/ice. One group preferred the rockier area that was free of ice. They had sleek black jackets on and were the smaller of the three species. Another group stood tall and had golden plumage around their neck and head. The third variety were in between those two groups and had little chin straps around their heads, making it look like they wore helmets.

"This must be their breeding season," he said. "There are lots of nests down there with either an egg or young." Tuatu came and looked out the window beside him. She got close enough that he felt her heat through his skin. Giving her a sidelong glance he didn't move, wanting to see if she would stay or pull away.

"Those young birds are adorable. I wonder if they can be humbled and handled?"

"For what purpose?"

"Companionship."

"Are you lonely, Captain?"

She looked at him quizzically. Why did he use her rank instead of name, she thought to herself. "A little," she admitted. "It would be nice to have company."

"I suspect those cute baby birds get large quickly."

"You're right of course. I guess I need to find a different kind of companion."

Now Ureth looked directly at her. He saw her smile mischievously and knew it to be an invitation. Since he was close enough to kiss her, he turned his head and lightly touched his lips to hers holding just a heartbeat before pulling back. The heat he felt lit a fire in the pit of his stomach, but he waited.

Tuatu had been flirting, so she expected his advances. But she had not expected the intensity of her own reaction. She felt a fire spark to life in her loins and her lips twitched and suddenly she shivered as if cold, but instead felt the fire rise up her spine and darken her throat and up her cheeks.

"Your blush looks lovely on you," he said quietly. The heat in his eyes made her want to remove the clothes she was wearing, but they weren't alone and she didn't want to rush anything. Instead, she looked down, her lashes brushing her cheeks and allowed the smile inside to crease her lips.

"That was lovely too," she answered just as quietly.

When she looked him directly in the eye, she reached her hand up to his face, glanced quickly toward the front, then closed the distance to kiss him. This time, it wasn't brushing, but full contact. She tasted his breath, it was spicy. He invited her to come in, drawing her into his warmth, as he explored hers. For a Shard there was nothing else in their world but each other, the sensations of their mouths, and their tongue's discovery. The tiny nick in her lip gave her a thrill as she tasted a drop of his venom.

A nearly inaudible knock broke the moment as Wendell cleared his throat. "Ahem, sorry to interrupt, but we seem to have run out of ground below us."

Ureth broke the kiss first, slowly, as if he was waking up from a very deep sleep. Feeling dazed and dizzy, Tuatu pulled away, and realized that it was more than just a kiss. She instinctively shook her head as if to clear her thoughts, "Ah, thank you Wendell. Why don't you put us down somewhere and we can get out?" she said.

"I cannot do that."

"Oh? Why not?"

"Because there is no land under the ice. And that ice doesn't look all that stable."

"Return to where the scanner said there was land and put her down please, Wendell."

Turning back to Ureth, he whispered to her, "My, that was "

"Yes, it was," said Tuatu, putting a finger delicately on his lips. "Um, shall we focus on this trip?"

"Now, I don't want to," Ureth said. It was his turn to be a little roguish.

"Too bad! This was your idea," she said, giggling.

The shuttle started dropping, and touched down on the ice, the engines whirring down and stopping. They heard Wendell switching things off. "Do you want me to leave the life support systems running?"

"Are you sure we are on solid land here?" asked Ureth.

"According to the scan, yes. There are about three Avens of ice and then solid land under the ship. But be careful wandering out over that ice. It's nothing but water under it."

"We will. Considering the planet has so much water, unlike our homeworld, we probably need to learn how to survive it," said Tuatu.

"That is a much different project," said Ureth. "Come on, let's get going. Step carefully everyone. We don't want to end up in that water."

"VIRA, keep the shuttle engaged and ready for flight."

"Do you mean the heat?" she asked. "Yes, will do. We'll want it warm inside when we return."

Wendell came to the back and the three of them put on their gear, helmets, and each picked up a ruck sack of tools and instruments to take measurements and record data.

Disembarking first, Tuatu said, "I'll take the geography measurements."

"Conversion mode available, though your units are more elegant, Captain," said VIRA. "I'll be monitoring you while you're out on the ice."

"Thank you, VIRA."

"Excellent, I'll go and explore life forms. Wendell, will you come and help me, just in case I need a pair of hands to help bring things back?"

"Yes, Ureth."

Tuatu got out the scanning devices. One used two forms of penetrating radar that allowed them to see deep underground. On Zydee, it allowed them to find the faults in the rock before they shifted dangerously. It also allowed them to create detailed maps of the ground and find seams of minerals and lava tubes. She was going to use this device now to map underground to find as much as she could.

It turned out, Wendell had landed them within two

Traverses of the sea a manageable distance for a mapping loop. Tuatu planned her route methodically: from the ship to the coast (two Traverses or two thousand paces), then five Veylen (or five hundred paces) along the shoreline, before arcing inland to parallel her first path and returning to complete a rectangular survey.

The ground she would cover formed a clean three-dimensional map to a depth equal to the crater where Arieveth now rested.

["Our Traverse," VIRA explained quietly through the console's display, "is 1,000 strides. One Aven equals one stride. One Veylen equals one hundred strides. Conversion mode available if preferred."]

"Thank you VIRA. For now, I'll stick to my regular measurements."

Wendell carried a large sack that contained a small portable laboratory. It would allow him to take samples of the ice and label them as he went. "What are you looking for?" asked Wendell.

"I'm looking for life forms," said Ureth. "If the Oorithi survive here, what else does, and what do they eat?"

"I think I saw them eating animals from the sea," said Wendell.

"Really? What did they look like?"

"Silvery floppy things. Maybe we can catch them ourselves."

"Let's go!" The two of them set off for the blue water they could see in the distance. As they got closer a deafening squawking sound filled the air. Then a stench like nothing they've ever smelled hit their noses."

"Oh my gods! What is that horrible stink?"

"That I believe is Oorithi feces and urine, you're smelling. I'm not surprised it is strong. Look at how many individuals there are here! There must be millions of them!"

As the men got to the top of a rise, the sea came into clear view. The men proceeded along the top of the ridge until they were close to the colony of birds. The birds were between the men and the sea. It was wall-to-wall birds, all talking, all flapping their flippers, and packed in very close; not more than a body length between them. The tallest of the birds was about waist height on the men, so they were pretty big.

"Let's see how close we can get to them, shall we?" asked Ureth excitedly. They cautiously walked toward the birds, trying to appear non-threatening. The birds never flinched. They watched them approach and went back to talking.

"Clearly we don't look like predators to them. I wonder who predates them?"

"Do you think they're talking?"

"Of course they are. Look at them. They are clearly communicating with each other. Listen to the variety of sounds they make. They clearly have names for themselves and a unique call for each parent-chick pairing. It's a matter of what. Perhaps T'shaya will come up with something. Right now, can you pull out our video equipment and set it up for me? I'm going to get closer."

Wendell opened up the ruck sack and found the recording devices and set them up. Then he found a snack in the bag too, so he sat down to watch and eat.

Ureth quietly and slowly walked closer to the birds. Once he was a body length from them he kneeled down in the snow and sat still. A bird separated itself from the crowd and walked toward him, stopping a half-length away. At that distance the bird was nearly as tall as Ureth while he kneeled. They were at eye-level. The bird started talking to him, tilting its head first to the right, then to the left, repeated itself and then staring right at him.

Ureth didn't know what to do, so he mimicked the sound as best as he could and mimicked the head movements.

The bird's eyes opened wider then it squawked again, but differently.

Ureth again mimicked the bird. This time with both sounds, but pointed to himself and said his name while hitting himself.

The bird nodded at him. Bobbing its head quickly up and down, then stretching its neck straight up and gave a curious long low whistle. The bird finished up by looking straight at Ureth again. Then it waddled over and made some soft sounds, almost a cooing, and then plunked itself down beside the man on its belly.

"I think you have been selected as a mate, Ureth," said Wendell chuckling.

"You think so?" he asked, looking at the bird quietly chuckling himself. "You may be right." He reached out his hand to touch the bird's head but instead, laid it flat on the ground in front of it. The bird looked up at him and he could have sworn it smiled. "I don't want to give it the wrong impression."

"Well, just don't bring it any rocks then."

"Rocks? Why rocks?"

"I've been observing that one of the rituals is one mate brings rocks to the other to build a nest. I believe it's the male who does the rock bringing while the female does the nest building."

"So this must be a female bird."

"It would seem so," said Wendell.

"She is rather pretty. Her eyes are striking. I think I'll call her Tiki."

"Who's rather pretty?" asked Tuatu, approaching them from behind.

"You've finished your scans already?" asked Ureth.

"Yes. What have you found?"

"This," said Ureth pointing to the bird lying beside him, "is a female Oorithi, and it seems that she has chosen me as a mate."

"Start bringing Tiki rocks then," said Tuatu. "She'll want the largest nest from the largest male on the beach." Tuatu burst out laughing. The bird was slightly startled at this display, and apparently took it as a challenge. Tiki got up and waddled away quickly.

Wendell then started laughing. "Oh my, Captain, you challenged her and won! Now you're the mated female!"

Her cheeks suddenly burned with heat and Tuatu turned away from the men and looked at the horizon to hide her reaction. It was easier to be Captain than Thiopeta, thought Tuatu.

"Thiopeta would have wanted more," said Ureth.

The horizon gave her nothing. Her ruse was hollow, she couldn't even point out a stone.

Keeping her face averted until she felt the heat die down, she realized that she sort of liked the idea of being mated to Ureth. Did she challenge the female bird unconsciously?

"Come team, let's continue our exploration of this beach," said Ureth. "There are lots more species to document."

"Wait a shard," said Wendell, his voice rising. "What's this? Under the ice?"

VIRA Interim Log:

I am sensing changes from the Captain and Ureth. What do they mean? Their body chemistry alters whenever they are in close proximity. This requires more observation.

As they were walking, Ureth pointed out an interesting phenomenon green ice. "I believe this ice has microscopic plants growing in it, called algae. The algae comes from the water, and has learned how to thrive in the cold ice. I'll take a sample of this for research, Wendell."

"Captain?" said VIRA into Tuatu's comm.

Wendell stepped up and cut a section of the ice that was green and stored it in a thermal box.

"What did you find on the scans, Captain?" Ureth used her rank in front of Wendell so he didn't look too personal. Tuatu touched her comm unit and responded to VIRA. "Go ahead VIRA."

"My scans are picking up a very large animal under

the ice shelf."

"Acknowledged VIRA." She stepped back to Ureth.

"I have to analyse the scans back at the ship, but I believe I found several other volcanoes, at least one is apparently active, and has quite the heat signature," said Tuatu.

"Even through the ice? Was there ice on top of it?"

"Oh yes, they were all completely covered in ice. Readings indicated that the ice is approximately four and a half Traverses thick. It completely covered the mountain, but there was a strange cylindrical vent above it that was steaming. I'd like to collect some of those gases to find out what sort of emissions it has."

"I'll make sure we get that sample," said Wendell.

"Captain," said VIRA, now broadcasting to all three of them. "The object under the ice is a very large creature."

"What sort of creature, VIRA?" asked Wendell.

"It appears to have a very long streamlined body with eight arms. I'm not sure. I will search our archives. This creature seems familiar somehow. I've estimated its length to be as long as three Veylens."

"Three hundred strides! That is monstrously large!"

The small group of explorers had walked another

Veylen when clouds appeared and started snowing.

"Snow? Isn't this a summer season?"

"It is, but I suspect on this land mass, snow is possible at any time of year. It's light so it won't hinder us."

The closer they got to the water the more heavily the snow fell. The air turned sharp and hollow, like it had been emptied of sound. Even the squawks of the Oorithi had grown distant, muffled under the weight of the stormfront rolling in behind them.

Tuatu adjusted the collar of her thermal suit and scanned the horizon. "This is different," she murmured.

Ureth paused beside her. "The silence?"

She nodded. "Even the wind has gone still." She suddenly had a long shiver run up her back. Something was wrong, and it wasn't obvious.

The group crested a low ridge overlooking a frozen tidal shelf. Ice cracked softly beneath their boots, echoing across the vast bay where floes drifted like broken puzzle pieces. Strange twanging noises could be heard and some strange staccato ones as well. Wendell was slightly ahead, his breath rising in white puffs as he scanned the terrain with a handheld bioscanner.

"Wait," Ureth said suddenly. "Do you feel that?"

The ground trembled barely, but it was there. A

rhythmic thrum, like something massive shifting beneath the ice. A sound reached them. It wasn't wind; it wasn't cracking ice. It was low, resonant almost a hum. Tuatu turned to VIRA's voice in her helmet.

"This is the object I picked up on my scan. Unclassified subsonic frequency detected. Biogenic in origin. Caution advised," said VIRA.

Wendell froze. "What was that?"

Ureth raised a hand. "Don't move." Out beyond the ice shelf, something rose.

Tuatu didn't speak, but she froze utterly. VIRA's voice came through their earpieces, low and reverent: "Unidentified terrestrial life form. Mass: approximately 4 Avens. Warning: apex predator traits detected."

Tuatu reached for her neck where a nasty scar was all that remained of an injury she received as a young woman. Memories of that hunt gone wrong plagued her dreams for many Silences, waking her up in a cold sweat. But that was so long ago, why would those thoughts come to mind now?

All three of them fell silent as they watched a shape start to emerge from the ice beyond the rise a pale shape, massive, regal, and slow-moving. At first glance, it looked like a cloud moving across the ice, until it turned and revealed eyes that burned amber in the sun.

"What is that?" Wendell whispered.

The shape coalesced into a a hill, or so it seemed, rising from the frozen expanse. But the hill moved again. The curve of it resolved into a massive, furred creature. As it emerged fully from the fracture in the ice, water cascaded from its pelt like a waterfall of stars.

"Our ancient texts record an animal very similar to this. It was an apex predator, preying even on Zydeans. They called it a Thalgarin. Heavily muscled, heavily furred, their skin was nearly impossible to pierce. Their claws are as long as your hand and sharp as a chef's knife. Quite deadly. They can also run fast, although they prefer to lumber slowly. Because they are the apex, they are slow to anger, but once they think you're food, they will hunt you until they get you," broadcast VIRA.

It stood fully upright nearly four Avens tall. Its fur was the color of starlit snow, rippling with a strange, silvery sheen that caught the ambient light. Eyes like twin glaciers locked onto them, glowing faintly with inner luminescence.

"By the Spiral," Ureth whispered. The creature didn't charge. It didn't roar. It simply stood, watching.

Tuatu's heart pounded, but she didn't look away. "Is it evaluating us?"

VIRA replied softly, "Local biosignature aligns with apex trophic level. Behavior: sentient or near-sentient. Caution: mythic attributes confirmed in Zydean oral recollections."

The creature had been moving toward them, but had stopped on a ridgeline, its nose lifting to catch their scent. It was at least as tall as two Zydeans and four times as broad. They could now see its fur was not pure white, but mottled in pale silver and stone, with stains of brown and grey on its underbelly, like the cliffs behind it. Its jaws spread wide in a yawn and then a howl that seemed dislocated from its throat.

The creature huffed and blew clouds of breath from its nostrils as though clearing them of water. Shaking itself violently, starting at the head, then the shoulders, torso, and flanks, then the back end, was a sight to behold as ice and water were flung in a great aurora of steam and droplets around it. Each droplet caught the sun and winked like a prism, creating a rainbow of color arching over it.

"It's beautiful," Ureth murmured. "Like something from an ancestral dream."

The bear considered them. Not aggressively. It blinked its eyes slowly. Almost solemnly. What was it thinking? Was it remembering something? Had it seen a Zydean before?

Huffing again, it turned and walked away, slowly as if bound by ritual. The Thalgarin stepped forward onto the shelf, each paw leaving a deep impression in the ice. It sniffed the air, then gave a long, deep vocalization a sound that wasn't quite a growl. It resonated in their bones.

The Oorithi in the distance went dead silent. Perky heads and bright eyes turned in their direction as one. Nothing moved.

Tuatu found herself stepping forward slowly, respectfully. The bear turned to watch her. She stopped, knelt down and removed one glove, held up her hand palm-out, and whispered her name aloud. "Thiopeta Tuatu."

The Thalgarin blinked once. Then it lifted its massive head to the sky and let out a sound unlike anything they had ever heard: a mournful, harmonic howl that seemed to echo across time itself.

After glancing down toward the Oorithi, it turned and lumbered back toward the sea. The Ice cracked and groaned and the Thalgarin was gone, vanishing into the white mist, like a memory receding into dream.

Silence again. Only now it felt full. Alive. Enduring. Then the chatter of the Oorithi resumed as if nothing had happened.

Ureth exhaled. "We weren't meant to conquer this world."

Tuatu nodded. "We were meant to listen. Let's get to the water before this snow traps us."

The group continued their walk to the sea.

The three of them stood ankle-deep in slushy meltwater, at the edge of what looked like a stable shelf of sea ice. It stretched out before them in irregular, jigsawed patterns, with leads of dark, glassy water meandering between the floes. Tuatu knelt at the edge of one such gap, scanner in hand, eyes narrowed from the glare off the water.

"Look for plant life," asked Ureth. "I'm hoping to find something edible."

Wendell was walking along the edge of the ice, when he suddenly dropped to his knees. "I've found something!"

Waving beneath the surface was a bioluminescent, wide green plant that had long tendrils with balloons attached. The tendrils held bunches of balloons keeping the plant upright in the water as it reached for the surface. It appeared to be glowing with a silvery light. "Isn't that spectacular! Grab me a sample please!" Wendell reached into the water, screamed momentarily at the frigid temperature, and grabbed onto the plant. With a strong tug, the whole thing came free and floated to the surface. He pulled it into a net that he had been carrying, then put it into a collapsible container with some of the water.

"We should give this a name," said Ureth. "Any suggestions?"

"How about Glowlace?" suggested Wendell.

"Sounds appropriate to me."

They also found some ice with a red tint and some string form of the green algae that they got samples of. Wendell was pulling something else from the water when he yelped mildly. "What do you have there?" asked Ureth.

"I don't know. But it looks like some kind of moss. It reacts with my skin when I pulled it from some rocks. It feels warm. And yes, I have samples."

"There's movement beneath," Tuatu said. "Slippery, fast tentacled, I think. Ureth, I think we found one of those squids Wendell saw earlier."

Wendell had already pulled out a collapsible net, clearly prepared for adventure. "I brought this for just such a moment."

Tuatu gave him a sidelong look. "Good, you brought a net."

"They look strange, a pointed body, and what's with all the arms? I count eight of them!"

Ureth chuckled. "Let's try to catch one, then study it before it disappears back into the void. I'll grab a container to put it in that will hold water."

They crept closer to the water's edge, peering into the ink-black slit between the ice sheets.

"Ah Captain, I need to caution you. The seabed drops off there very quickly. Within a few paces there is nothing under the ice but water."

The water was impossibly clear, revealing sinuous flashes of something iridescent. The creatures moved like liquid thought too fast for the eye, yet leaving a trace of presence in the mind.

Tuatu reached for her scanner again, but just as she did, the edge of the ice under her boots shifted slightly.

She froze.

"Was that ?" she began, but the question was answered by the sudden lurch beneath their feet.

The entire sheet of ice they stood on gave a long, groaning creak... and began to move.

"Wait," Ureth said calmly. "Did this just detach from the land?"

"It appears," said Wendell, far less calmly. "we're drifting."

The wind had picked up. The floe slid like a whisper into the current, pulling them away from the shore. The land was receding, much faster than you'd think possible. A scattering of seabirds rose in alarm overhead.

"Captain, I tried to warn you."

"Yes VIRA, and now we're on a floating ice cube!"

Tuatu turned slowly to look at them both. "So,

according to VIRA, we're floating on the ocean. Over unknown depths. Following an eight-armed creature with a pointed head that swims really, really fast?"

"I think it's following us," said Ureth, pointing.

"Captain, I recommend that all of you remain in the centre of the ice floe." I think they're ignoring me, observed VIRA.

Sure enough, a large creature had surfaced beside the ice, its head and mantle a mottled shimmer of blues and greens. It blinked one massive eye at them then squirted a jet of water straight into Wendell's face.

"That felt personal," Wendell spluttered.

Tuatu laughed genuinely laughed as she pulled her hood back over her head. "It was personal. We're the strange species here."

They floated like that for several long moments. The sun glinted off the open water. The world was silent except for the occasional creak of the ice and the gentle hiss of waves beneath them.

"This ocean is... massive," Ureth murmured. "That's a lot of water! You cannot see an end to it."

"No, it's unnerving, isn't it? We don't have water like this at home."

"Not since the Cracking, no," said Tuatu. "It was mostly burned off. It is why our world was dying water is a life-giving substance, and without it, life doesn't thrive. It may learn how to adapt, but eventually it withers and dies."

"I wonder how far it goes?" asked Wendell.

"This planet is mostly water," answered VIRA, through their helmets. "There are 1.386 billion cubic Traverses of water on this planet, with 92.7% being salty sea water."

"That's a lot of water!" said Wendell.

"I said that already," joked Ureth. "VIRA, how deep is this sea?"

"The average depth of the oceans on this planet is 3,682 Avens. The depth of the sea surrounding this continent The Southern Ocean is 7,236 Avens. It's one of the deepest oceans."

"All the more reason to be careful then."

Tuatu nodded. "Nothing like Zydee. We had no concept of endless water. This is a living body of its own."

"Zydee would have called this a god."

"Maybe Earth still does."

Eventually, the tide shifted again. The ice floe bumped softly into a thicker ridge of land-fast ice. With careful steps and some awkward leaping, they made their way back to shore Wendell clutching a dripping scanner and Tuatu carrying a sample container that held one small, bioluminescent tentacle.

"Congratulations," Ureth said as they regained solid ground. "We've caught part of the creature, floated on a mobile platform of frozen water, and been mocked by aquatic invertebrates."

"What shall we call it?" asked Wendell.

"The squid?" Wendell asked, wringing out his sleeves.

Tuatu glanced at the specimen and smiled. "Inqualin. That'll be its name. It means surprise beneath stillness.' Very Zydean."

"A squid, because it squirts," said Ureth.

"We'll call it the Drift Event," Tuatu said.

They stood in silence for a long time, listening to the ocean breathe.

After drifting and bobbing in the water for some time, the team sat on the ice listening to the wind, waves, and the occasional creature jump out of the water and splash.

Oorithi were hunting under the waves and coming up with fish in their mouths. They watched the Zydeans drifting on the floe with approval, as if that's what ice floes were for.

A very large creature, maybe as long as one Veylen, hurled its entire body out of the water and belly flopped on the surface, sending a huge wave rushing at them. They had to all lie down for fear of being knocked off the ice.

Another of those creatures surfaced just an Aven away from the edge of their floe. Its single, curious eye regarded the strangers with great intelligence.

Tuatu instinctively reached out with her mind and hand, to try to communicate with this obviously sentient creature, but it disappeared beneath the waves and reappeared dozens of Veylen away. And then an image, complete, three dimensional, and detailed, popped into her head showing the location the whale was going. Had she known this planet better, she would have been able to find it. Was this creature reaching out like the Thalgarin seemed to have?

"Wow, they can swim fast!" she remarked. Out of the stillness they hadn't noticed, a low hum approached from the southern sky, rising above the hiss of the wind and lapping water. Tuatu shaded her eyes as a dark silhouette swept into view over the ice: their shuttle, gleaming in the sun like a metal beetle, skimming just meters above the ice floes.

VIRA's voice crackled in their headsets, dry and amused. "Captain. It appears I can't leave you alone for long. Shall I chart this as an unscheduled voyage?"

Tuatu pressed her comm. "Please log it under: accidental marine incompetence."

"Logged. Rescue protocols engaged."

The shuttle gently descended a few meters ahead, extending its side ramp with a soft hiss. A targeting laser marked their floe's edge, and small maneuvering jets fired, nudging the shuttle perfectly in line with the drifting ice.

"Hop on!" Wendell shouted, already jogging awkwardly across the uneven surface.

Ureth helped Tuatu up, and she turned once at the shuttle threshold, looking back at the sea. The Inqualin had vanished, leaving only faint ripples and the memory of its curious gaze.

She boarded.

Inside, the warmth embraced them. The ramp was sealed. The engines hummed louder as the shuttle pulled up and away from the drifting sheet below.

"Welcome back," said VIRA, as they peeled away from the ice and rejoined the sky. "I took the liberty of warming your boots."

Tuatu sat heavily in her chair, water dripping from her gloves, and smiled. "Add this to our logbook: The ocean is not to be underestimated."

"Already done, Captain. Subtext added: "The

Inqualin awaits."

"Among many other things, VIRA." She glanced at Ureth, who was still holding the sample vial like it was made of starlight. "Let's get this home."

Tuatu's Log: Silence 33, Cycle 04

An errant thought occurred to me while I was returning to the ship after our expedition. What if that pod we found was from a previous exodus from our planet. Could our planet have had more than one catastrophic event? Could we have fled our planet before?

It's just a thought. I will put more effort into this another day, but I wanted to log it here.

Chapter 14
Return and Intimacy

[SILENCE — CYCLE 07]

The shuttle slipped back into the mountain like a returning thought. Hidden apertures opened with quiet precision, sealing behind them as the docking bay pressurized and warmed.

Tuatu, Ureth, and Wendell stepped down into the familiar glow of the bay's biolights. It was oddly grounding the scent of clean polymer, the soft click of their boots on reinforced stone. VIRA dimmed the lights gently as they passed through the decontamination mist.

"Welcome home," she said. "Shall I alert the bio-sciences team?"

"Just T'shaya," Tuatu answered. "I'd rather this be... small, for now."

They walked together through the curving

passages, Tuatu cradling the Inqualin sample in a temperature-stabilized vial with sea-water. The creature's tissue if it could even be called that shifted slowly inside, glowing faintly green and violet in pulses. It looked like translucent strands of root and muscle braided together, constantly rearranging themselves.

Even in death, it was... not still.

"Do you feel like it's watching us?" Wendell asked quietly.

"It doesn't have eyes," said Ureth.

"Still."

T'shaya met them in the lower lab, her outer robe tossed hastily over a sleepshift. Her silver hair was caught in a loose tie, and her fingers twitched before she even reached them already eager to begin.

"You found something. Oooo let me see!"

Tuatu handed over the vial. "It tried to touch us. I think it was curious."

T'shaya turned the vial slowly in her hands. "This isn't like anything in our databases. The tissue structure is semi-crystalline. It isn't dissolving it's self-repairing. That's not just resilience, it's some kind of adaptive morphology. Look! The skin is changing color!"

"Could it think?" asked Ureth.

"To determine that I'll need the whole organism. Can you get one?" T'shaya looked up. "Give me a little time, I'll know more. But yes it might have been more than just an animal."

"It does resemble some of the most ancient species in the Zydean archives," said VIRA. "In fact, I searched through everything we have and it appears to be a Cephalopod and perhaps linked to the ones here on this planet."

As they stood in the lab, Tuatu glanced at the holo display behind T'shaya. It was showing an old scan of Zydee's freshwater oceans tiny, enclosed bodies of water teeming with microbial life, strictly regulated, precious. Nothing in her life had prepared her for a sea that moved, breathed, and hunted.

She turned to Ureth. "We weren't alone out there."

He nodded. "We never were. May I walk you to your quarters, Captain?"

"That would be nice, Ureth. Thank you. And please, call me Thiopeta."

"I shall endeavour to do that when we're alone." They snaked their way through the corridors and across the open spaces where the colonists had set up agriculture and recreational areas. They went up many floors, and worked their way to the front end of the ship where the Captain's quarters were located. Once there the two of them stopped.

"I'd like to continue the conversation we started on the shuttle," said Tuatu.

"I'd like that very much," answered Ureth. "Do you have time?"

"I don't have anything to do," she said as she opened the door with a wave of her hand. The embedded chip in her wrist carried all her identification data, so that she could effortlessly enter any room in the ship. She was one of a few people who could do that. Most people were restricted in some way to what they could get access to. The crew was given access to whatever they were hired to work on, plus their own quarters, and recreational areas and common areas.

Citizens were not allowed anywhere on the ship that was functional to the operation of the ship; only common areas and their own quarters. If they were involved with one of the many jobs that contributed to the welfare of the colony, they had access to relevant parts of the ship.

The two entered Tuatu's apartment. The security greeted her and her guest, acknowledging Ureth was there and logging the entry. Tuatu walked over to her view screen and gazed out.

There wasn't much to see inside the crater, just the beautiful layers of ice that formed the walls, but at certain parts of the day, those walls glistened with rivulets of water running down them, or rays of reflecting starshine that winked on and off. When the star shone into the crater, the ice danced with colors and looked like jewels had been embedded deep in the curves of the ice. Rainbows connected across cracks as the light refracted on the cubist fractures.

Tuatu wrung her hands together, and her shoulders were held high and tight.

Ureth followed her over to the view screen and gently laid his hands on her shoulders, massaging them until he felt the tension ease somewhat. "Are you nervous?" he asked.

"A little," admitted Tuatu. "It's been a long time since I was with someone."

"We don't have to do anything, I'd just like to spend some time with you."

"Why don't I make something to eat? It will give my hands something to do."

"I can make some suggestions for your hands." Ureth leered for a moment before dispelling it with a wide grin.

Tuatu prepared a meal for the two of them, and brought it to the lounge where Ureth was seated. Handing him a plate, she sat beside him. A moment later, she bounced back up nervously, and walked back to the food prep area and opened the fridge door. "Would you like a beverage?" she asked.

"What do you have?"

"I have a bottle of Virellan left. It's an old one, but it should be fine. The liquid has aged beautifully and has a fine smooth texture. My family had a vineyard and made their own blend.

"That sounds wonderful. What is it? "

Tuatu selected two thin-walled, spiraled glass vessels from her shelf and poured out half glasses of the Virellan, a beverage prized by Zydeans. It was originally a sacred ferment consumed only during rites of passage or bonding ceremonies. It was believed to align one's internal Spiral Zydean life energy with the cosmic rhythm of time. Over time, it became a celebratory drink, still treated with reverence.

It had a nose of smoky plum, starlight spice, trace minerals, and faint ozone with a rich caramelized stone fruit taste, a touch of fire-root heat, and a lingering ashwood bitterness. But the finish was warm, resonant, and strangely grounding as if one's blood briefly remembers an ancestral frequency.

She walked over to Ureth and handed him a glass ceremoniously. "They say Virellan can only be served in vessels that reflect light into a pattern symbolizing the twin moons of Zydee."

"Oh really? And do these do that?" He raised his glass and looked through the clear amber liquid and the spiral glass, and he could swear he saw two moons.

"There is a traditional way to honor the Virellan."

"And what is that?" he asked. She stepped very close to him and brought her hand up behind his head and bent it down to hers ever so gently, until their foreheads touched. "Resonai'veth may our spirals sing in harmony," she murmured. Then Tuatu drank the entire glass. Ureth straighten up, watched her with a twinkle in his eye and drained his glass as well.

"Oh that is smooth," remarked Ureth. He set the glass down and involuntarily growled. A slight wobble hit his head as he realized that it was indeed potent. "Oh that is intense!" he said as he touched his tongue to his fangs that were starting to tingle.

Happy for the slight inebriation, it calmed his own nerves. He laughed inwardly at himself for feeling nervous. He felt like he was back home and a young man again. But this woman kept him on his toes. She was exciting and mysterious. He didn't know much about her, and he intended on remedying that.

Tuatu watched him drain his glass and smiled. That would slow him down a bit, she thought. She couldn't believe she was feeling like a nervous cadet. Her stomach was fluttering like it had an entire hive of bees flying around inside. But it wasn't fear, it was anticipation.

She was noticeably excited for the possibility that lay ahead. She just had to play it cool; not move too quickly; not be too eager; not be too fast.

Tuatu continued to sip her drink. She felt it hit her head too, and the room suddenly shifted. She felt hot and needed to get out of her uniform. "Um Ureth, do you mind if I get changed? This uniform is not the most comfortable to relax in."

"But of course. Please do. I'll get the fireplace started and make it comfortable here."

She looked at him out of the periphery of her vision, wondering what he would consider comfortable. As she walked to her sleeping room, she saw him picking up some pillows and arranging them on the floor in front of the fireplace.

When she emerged from her room, Ureth was pleased to see she had changed to a loose, flowing robe that moved with the air swirling around her legs as she walked. It was a lightweight fabric, nearly translucent and it formed to her body when she stopped moving. It gave him a surge in his nether regions he hadn't expected.

Ureth had filled their glasses again, and was reclining against the pillows. Tuatu joined him on the floor, feeling the warmth of the flames on her face. They were fake flames, because they couldn't actually have a fire inside the ship, but it was very realistic with sound, heat, and light. It was a perk of being the captain to have a fireplace in her apartment.

"So have you always been in the military?" Ureth started the conversation off. He squinted his eyes to focus himself on her face as he felt his vision wander down her body.

"No, it's my third career."

"Your third career? What did you do before?" Ureth envisioned her as

"I've always been in a service. How about you?"

"I'm a scientist. I've always been a scientist. At first, my field of interest was trying to find a solution to providing water for the ark ships. Then it became about sustainability. Now, it's more about genetics."

"What sort of genetics?"

"The kind that will see our people continue."

"Oh so creation and procreation."

"Yes, that's correct," he said. "When I learned that the humanoid species here were very close to ours, I wanted to run some studies to see if there is an evolutionary path with them. My observations suggest they are just too far behind right now. But I need to confirm that and do some more research. I need bodies."

"I suspect you're correct. They do seem pretty primitive. We'll just have to make do with ourselves, won't we?" She sipped her beverage. It was a wine-like beverage the ship created. "Mmmm, that's not bad."

"No, it's pretty good. It has quite the kick doesn't it?"

Thiopeta giggled a little, and Ureth thought it was a delightful sound. Like a babbling brook. "You have a lovely laugh. I want to hear more of that," he said.

"Then make more jokes," she answered with a smile.

"May I kiss you again? I quite liked the one we shared on the shuttle."

"It was quite nice." Tuatu leaned over to plop a kiss on his lips, but before she could pull away, his arm was wrapped around her back, trapping her there. The kiss went on and deepened. They broke a Shard later, Tuatu was panting and a flush had colored her cheeks.

Still in his arm, she relaxed and let her weight fall into him. She rested her head on his shoulder, not speaking, getting her breath back. Her body was tingling with excitement, and she could barely contain it. He didn't need to know that though, and wanted to be nonchalant.

Ureth's heart was racing and the adrenaline was pumping through him. Some ancient ritual was awakening in him, and he was desperately trying to tamp it down before it got out of hand. The ancient ritual was taking a woman as mate. He had been surprised with the intensity of the kiss, the intensity of the feelings that burst from him, and how his body was reacting. He tried to dismiss it as it's been too long' but this was very different.

Silently, he considered the woman leaning against him. He could feel every breath she took, noticed how she was panting, and how warm her skin was. He heard her heart race even as his own blood was in his ears. He felt her excitement like an energy that leaped to close a circuit, sizzling him and bonding her to him. Was this it? Was this the bond?

Tuatu listened to his chest, she could hear his breathing, not labored, but heavy like he was keeping something in. His heart was thumping loudly, pumping blood through him in greater volumes than normal. And she picked up the scent; the scent of arousal, of power, of bonding. She knew that scent, because she had bonded before, but her mate had been killed. She hadn't believed she would bond again. But there it was, that unmistakable scent of a man ready. Does he know it?

She went to sit up, but she suddenly felt his other arm pull her hips over so she was on top of him.

She stilled.

He felt the stillness. "This is a line we cannot uncross, so there is no rush if you want to stop."

She gazed down into his eyes, considering his offer. and saw there a mirror of her own feelings, desires, and emotions. She relaxed, and came into full contact with him. She felt his hands slide up her spine, caressing her, running through her hair, drawing it back from her face. She was intimately aware of his body beneath her. The bones in his hips, how they balanced perfectly under her hips. She rose when his diaphragm expanded and fell when it contracted beneath hers as he drew breath, and felt the warmth of it on her neck as he exhaled.

A heat was building between her legs, one that wouldn't be denied. She lifted her head and placed her hands on the pillows on either side of him for support. When she kissed him this time, it was not going to be short.

Ureth felt his fangs start to drop as her kiss lit a fire in his soul. He also felt her fangs and teased them with his tongue and was rewarded with a small sound of arousal. Tuatu explored him with her tongue, caressing his fangs and causing shudders as the sensitive protrusions reacted. Their fangs, once used for hunting, were now much more useful during lovemaking. They were an erogenous zone on both males and females, being very sensitive to touch.

The problem was, first sex between couples was usually rather rough, and ritualized. It represented the bonding and didn't happen without ceremony. Rarely did two Zydeans mate spontaneously. These feelings, this imperative had come on both of them without warning, and were so intense, they were not prepared to stop it.

Still connected by their kiss, Ureth growled in his throat and Thiopeta answered him with a purr. One second they were stretched out together on the pillows, and the next he was behind her and on top. He had her by her neck and was biting into the fleshy muscle of her shoulder. Thiopeta was moaning with pleasure as the venom coursed through her.

Ureth one moment was aware of what was happening they were kissing deeply, and the next he was on top of her biting her like an animal. As suddenly as it happened, Ureth broke the bite and rolled away and sat up. "Oh my, I'm so sorry, I apologize, Thiopeta. I didn't give you a choice to consent. I'm mortified at my behavior."

Thiopeta, still enjoying the venom in her blood, had a very contented smile on her face. She opened her eyes and looked at Ureth, not with condemnation, but with adMivvation. Ureth was baffled. "Ureth, I read the signs, I knew this was going to happen. And frankly, I am glad it did. May I pleasure you too?"

His breath caught and he coughed self-consciously.

"I would be honored to bring you pleasure," she said with a sultry seductive voice high on venom. He was so close to her when she said that, he could feel the heat coming off her. His excitement was real, and his fangs were eager. It had been so long since either of them had

had real pleasure. Thiopeta pulled him back down to her, pulling his ear with her lips. Gently nibbling the outside edge and using her tongue in the grooves caused a violent shudder from Ureth as his arousal went another notch up. She could now smell his sex.

"Don't do that unless you want me to jump you," he said. "That is a particular weakness of mine."

Thiopeta purred as she licked the grooves of his ear again, and pricked his lobe with her fang.

Ureth growled as she bent her head to his shoulder with her fangs fully elongated and bit down. The sweet nectar she delivered caused Ureth to experience the ultimate pleasure. Entwined in each other's bodies, Thiopeta said, "now we've started a conversation. But we need fewer clothes."

Outside the walls of Arieveth, snow had begun to fall summer or not. As if the world itself had paused to whisper: There is more beneath the surface.

Tuatu was working on a three dimensional map based on the data she had collected on their numerous field trips. She spent her time planning which locations they can use for geothermal energy. Ureth had made the point that if the volcanoes were single they could be ideal for habitat, providing it was no longer active.

It had been a few cycles since that amazing night with Ureth. The two of them had spent a lot of time together but none of it alone. That meant her mind was preoccupied with thoughts of his hands whenever she worked alone; playing the night over and over again. After her bonded mate died, she was always driven by task and accomplishment. She had forgotten that companionship was so rewarding; even in small amounts.

Ureth's role as a Commander made them equal in stature so they had similar experiences dealing with people. Both of them were also scientists in addition to their responsibilities. No one was just one thing in their society. Everyone had multiple talents and contributed in a variety of ways to the community.

Nevril, who had been busy with the construction of the power plant, the space port, and other facilities in the mountain, interrupted her thoughts. "Captain, I came to learn what you discovered on your field trip," he said, walking into the room.

"You're just in time, Nevril. The map should be almost ready to view." As they watched, a fully annotated three dimensional map of the continent, their location, and the data collected recently all appeared floating in front of them. Tuatu was able to interact with the map, spin it, rotate it, split it, flip it over, whatever she wanted to do.

"Data from several sources is represented here," said Tuatu. "The white outline is what we scanned from space. We can see the outline of the continent and the extent of the ice. You see this long arm spinning off the north western corner of the landmass? We want to travel up that way next because it's possibly connected to the landmass further north."

"There may have been a land bridge there at one time," said Ureth. "I wonder if we can find any evidence of that. Perhaps that is how the Thalgarin came to this continent."

"That seems a reasonable theory," said Tuatu. "There is no way a land animal of that size evolved on this continent. All the seabirds and seals would have migrated here by sea most likely."

"Those yellow lines must represent what I scanned yesterday," said Nevril. "You can see off this coast there are a number of volcanoes, and two appear to have some activity, two appear quiet, and two others appear dormant. Those mountains, the largest apparently on this land, are on the edge of a plateau that runs the entire width of the landmass, and extends into that arm."

"It appears the west side of this continent is slamming into the east side," said Tuatu. "However, this shows the west side is mostly ice, while the east side is all land with a thick layer of ice on top."

I suspect that a land bridge was formed as a result of that continental drift, and that the mountains are in fact an island chain as opposed to a landmass," said Nevril. "The surface ice makes it difficult to determine at this range. I'll have VIRA do more detailed scans when she is there."

"I want to continue our exploration of this land. My goal is to map all the volcanoes," Tuatu said. "My next trip, I want to head north along that peninsula and see what we can find. If our off-world scans are accurate, this volcanic chain goes all the way to the northern tip of this continent."

"When do you want to leave?" asked Ureth.

"How about three or four Spirals?"

"Sounds good. Should we bring Wendell?"

"I can fly this time," she said, grinning. "Besides, we don't really need a third person there do we?"

Ureth smiled deeply. Nevril was puzzled by that exchange, but chose to say nothing. Shaking his head he wandered away, leaving Tuatu and Ureth gazing into each other's eyes.

Chapter 15
The Song Under the Ice

[Silence 35 — Cycle 01]

The second expedition was packed and ready to leave at sunrise, several Spirals later. Tuatu was waiting for Ureth on board the shuttle. They had packed more food this time, as well as other containers and traps, in the event that they were able to find wildlife they could return with. Tuatu had reserved a large shuttle craft, capable of carrying two regiments of troops. It had on-board facilities to keep those people alive for an extended period of time.

As Ureth approached the shuttle, Tuatu felt a momentary thrill. "Keep it together Tuatu, you can't let yourself get distracted!" she chastised herself.

"Permission to come aboard, Captain?" asked Ureth.

"Permission granted."

Ureth brought several large cases with him, and had a couple of people help him stow his gear away in the back. Thanking them for their help, he shut the hatch of the ship and gave Tuatu the go ahead to lift off.

They flew in silence for a long while before Ureth said, "you're looking well today, Captain."

"Are you feeling awkward Ureth?" she asked. "Please don't. We're just two people on a mission."

"But we're not. Just two people, I mean."

"No, I suppose we're not," she admitted. They hadn't mated again since that first time. They hadn't really talked about it since. They had not had significant time alone. "Look, we haven't talked about what happened. I think we need to. Don't you?"

"Yes!" he said emphatically. "The intensity of our coupling took me by surprise. I hadn't expected to have such strong feelings at this stage of my life. I don't know what to do with them."

"I know what you mean. I was mated once. Bonded. He died in battle. I was empty for so long. I learned how to fill my life though, and found other things to interest me. Got involved in the military. I stopped looking for personal connections."

"I didn't know you had bonded before. That must have been a horrible time, loss. I'm sorry."

"It was a very, very, very, long time ago. No need to be sorry. I guess I was ready for intimacy again. And Ureth, I thoroughly enjoyed it. All of it."

"So did I," he said a little shyly. "I enjoyed it very much. In fact, I really want to be with you again. In every way."

"Now you know why I didn't think Wendell should come along."

"A wise woman, you are."

The shuttle resumed its travel until it reached the coast then turned northward. When the peninsula came into view, Tuatu set the craft down on the ice well back from the sea.

"I'll make sure the mapping computer has recorded our trip thus far." She got up from her seat and walked back to the computer station on the shuttle. The computer station duplicated almost all the technology that the ship had, but in a smaller size. It didn't scan as far, but it performed the same scans. The main system will be able to stitch all the smaller scans together to get a complete picture.

"Tuatu, come here!" called Ureth. When she got back to the cabin, he pointed out the window. There on a rise, was a Thalgarin. It had paused on a rise, lowering and turning its head slightly to look at them.

"When did he appear?"

"Just a moment before I called you. He just popped up out of nowhere."

"It's watching us again, not with hunger, not with fear but with recognition. Do you think it's the same animal we met the first time?"

"Perhaps. It certainly looks like the same one, I remember those eyes. They were like liquid silver, rimmed with dark rings." Those eyes now blinked slowly.

Tuatu whispered, "It's studying us, again."

"Perhaps. It certainly looks like the same one. I remember those eyes — liquid silver, rimmed with dark rings."

The creature blinked slowly, snow swirling around it in spirals, as though the world itself deferred to its presence.

Then, beneath the stillness, came another sound — low, rolling, almost too deep to hear. The ice beneath the shuttle trembled.

Ureth turned toward the viewport. "Did you feel that?"

"Yes." Tuatu adjusted the filters. Beneath the translucent ice, dark shapes moved in unison — vast, fluid, glowing faintly from within.

"Life forms," he said softly.

"The same harmonic frequency from orbit," VIRA confirmed over comms. "Identical sequence. Repeating."

"Whales," whispered Ureth. "They're gathering."

"Directly below the Thalgarin," VIRA added. "Perhaps drawn by its presence."

Tuatu stared out at the impossible scene — apex predator above, leviathans below — both silent, watching.

"It's as if they all knew we were coming," he said.

"Or," Ureth murmured, "as if we've finally come home."

VIRA waited a moment before speaking, her voice barely above the hum of the shuttle.

"Recording harmonic convergence," she said softly. Then, after a silence that almost sounded like thought:

"It feels... familiar."

Outside, the wind rose — carrying that same low vibration through the ice until it was impossible to tell whether it came from the whales, the world, or the ship itself.

Chapter 16
The Breath Between

"Do you think the Thalgarin sees us and not the ship?"

"No idea. Let's get out and see if we can approach."

"You don't think we're food?"

"No, because it's smart, and it would have attacked the last time if we had looked like food" They quickly got dressed into full gear, because it was 30 degrees below freezing, and dropped down to the snow from the hatch. Tuatu landed almost silently, but Ureth made a loud thump. That focused the Thalgarin's vision clearly.

It didn't growl. It didn't approach. Instead, it raised its broad muzzle and gave a low, echoing call that resonated through their chests. A note of mourning. Or warning.

Then, as silently as it had come, it turned. Each

stride covered distances no Zydean could have crossed unaided. It vanished into the white like a dream half-remembered.

Ureth exhaled. "We must document this."

Tuatu shook her head. "We must remember. Some beings are not meant to be studied. Not first."

She turned her eyes to the horizon, where the Thalgarin had disappeared. Snow began to fall, though it was still summer by their reckoning.

Ice sheet covered most of the tip of what looked like a hook of land jutting out into the sea. Beyond that hook were steep ruggedly cut mountains that stretched as far as the eye could see, like a spine all the way up the back of the land mass.

The further they went, the ice was breaking up in the water.

They could see the ice flowing down from the land into the water, where there were stretch marks as if this ice was a slow moving river.

They got to the end of the peninsula and saw a set of islands off shore to the west. One of the islands was covered by seabirds. They made a note of its location and decided they would fly over and take a closer look. The land here was wild, windswept, and lonely. There were no birds on this part of the peninsula. No one huddled in a group to stay warm. Clearly that was because this stretch of land jutting out into the sea was inhospitable to life. Winds whipped waves into a froth and then hurled them at the shore. The water froze on contact to create the most surreal looking structures they had ever seen.

Turning from the wind and looking directly at Ureth, she said, "I think we've seen all that we can on foot. We should make our way back to the shuttle." Her nose was bright red with a tiny white spot in the middle.

"Agreed. I think we need to get inside. Your nose is starting to freeze, literally. My fingers are numb in spite of the warming nature of the suit. I am looking forward to dinner."

Tuatu covered her face better to prevent the wind from biting her skin. They both turned around and trekked back toward the ship. They were further away than they realized, and by the time they arrived, they were both so stiff they could barely walk.

"We were dangerously close to hypothermia," said Tuatu once they were safe inside. "We cannot do that again. We got sidetracked and lost focus on the distance we went."

"I didn't realize we had gone as far as we had. I agree, we need to set a time limit if nothing else so that we know when we have to turn around," said Ureth. "Come here," he motioned to her. As she stepped closer, he wrapped his arms around her shoulders. "You're shivering!" He held her close, squeezing a bit to calm the shivers down, rubbing her arms and back. Eventually, her body stopped its shaking and she relaxed her head against his chest. When he felt her relax, he stepped away and looked into her face to check her nose.

"Your nose has recovered, too. Let's get something warm to eat."

They occupied themselves with cooking a simple hot meal and then making their version of a tea to sip. Tuatu pulled out a bottle of Virellan and added a dribble to their tea. That sent a small fire down her throat and she felt the warm aftermath all the way down. It warmed her in another way too, remembering what happened the last time they were drinking this spirit.

"That was a good idea!" said Ureth. "Now I feel warm all the way through." His eyes glowed with arousal. Ureth shifted slightly in his clothes as some other things came to life.

"You know, our instruments say it is 80 degrees below freezing out there with that wind! I'm amazed we made it back here!" said Tuatu, trying to keep it neutral. She fought with her instinct to assault him, to take him to the ground and ride him. Those baser instincts were more or less drilled out of them, centuries past. But strong emotions brought them back in a flash. She was having those strong emotions now. She swallowed against the urge rising in her throat, she took a deep breath and turned to him.

"Well, we'll definitely have to be more careful. I don't want to get lost out here," said Ureth. He looked at her, lips parted, her own eyes glowed slightly, and he knew that she felt the same as he. A self-satisfied feeling came over him, when he recognized that Tuatu wanted to take him as much as he wanted to take her.

They sat in a forced, companionable, silence, watching the wind blow the snow around outside. Once or twice they spotted the Thalgarin lumbering across the wasteland. The creature seemed to make a regular trip from the ocean edge to somewhere hidden from their view.

"That animal surely has antifreeze for blood! How does it survive in this cold?" asked Tuatu.

"Clearly, the animal has a thick layer of fat and a very dense fur coat. The fur also appears to be hydrophobic. Notice how it's never wet when it gets out of the water. That would be a very good adaptation for this environment. If you don't get wet, you won't get as cold."

The stilted, clinical conversation masked what was really going on in their minds. The energy built up like a tsunami and sparked in the space between them as they both fought their need.

"I'm feeling the Virellan," said Tuatu. "All that exercise "

"Do you want to rest? I'll take the first watch."

"Rest? That's the last thing I want."

"I'm feeling ," he said. Tuatu moved across the space and sat on the bench beside him. As he raised his hand to brush a strand of hair from her face, an electric shock took them by surprise. The sting of it was like a flare being lit.

In the next moment, they were rolling on the floor fighting for dominance, and Tuatu was winning. She had him on his back with his arms pinned above his head while she sat across his hips holding his body down.

The fire in her belly wasn't from the liquor any more. Her own fangs dropped, she gazed into his eyes and took the lead. Combat was physical, and so was their mating. At the end, glistening with beads of sweat around her hairline, breathing heavily, she flopped against his chest panting.

All she could feel was her skin on his and him connected to her. The venom coursing through both of them kept them high on their lovemaking for a long time.

Tuatu eventually grabbed a blanket from the storage compartment, and laid back down beside him, one leg flung over him. She covered them both, placed her head on his chest, and was asleep in moments. Ureth watched her for a few moments, before turning his attention back to the window. All their scanners were active, so if there was anything outside, he would be warned in advance. So he didn't need to worry.

Right now, he had the woman of his dreams by his side. Their bodies were so in tune, his heart had synchronized with hers during their combat. He listened to the two of them beating in unison. So this is what it's like to be mated and bonded," he thought to himself. I could get used to this.

210

Chapter 17
The Mother of Ice

The next morning, they woke up together as starshine came streaming in the other side's window.

"That was an eventful night," teased Tuatu. "Visitors?"

"Oh very, there were several visitors. I couldn't get any to stay though." Ureth grinned and got up to make their morning beverage. Tuatu admired his body, relaxed and warm from the night. She stretched like a cat on the floor, not taking her eyes from him, displaying herself too.

Ureth noticed. "If you want something, just ask."

Tuatu crooked her finger at him, and he was on the floor with her before she could speak. The morning beverage could wait.

"Mmm, thank you," she said, taking a cup of hot liquid from Ureth. It was a strong black beverage that gave a jolt to the system and helped wake you up. It had a bitter aftertaste.

"So what shall we do today?" he asked, sitting there unapologetically naked.

"Let's fly over the spot where we have seen the Thalgarin walking to and from. Perhaps there is a den in that location. Then I'd like to go over and look at that island."

"Sounds like a plan."

Within 30 shards, they were dressed, had eaten, and were off the ground. They had a little difficulty lifting off, because the sleds had frozen into the surface. However, a little burst from the engines and she separated nicely from the frozen tundra. After gaining some altitude, they started to fly toward the spot they think the Thalgarin went to. They were experiencing extremely strong winds that buffeted them around, making it difficult to control the flight. As a result, Tuatu was fighting the steering as the ship twitched and lurched back and forth and up and down. At one point, it felt like the ship was pushed down to the ground by an unseen hand as they felt the bottom drop out and the ground rush up toward them. Tuatu got it back under control, but there was a bead of sweat on her brow from the strain of fighting the steering column.

Tuatu discovered that there was a small hollow at the base of a small hill on the leeward side. She maneuvered the shuttle in behind the hill, and the wind disappeared.

"Wow, that's effective! I can land here. Shall I?"

"Not yet. How far up can you get before we hit the wind again?"

"Perhaps a few aven. Let me try. The ship rose up again slowly, until Tuatu felt the wind start to buffet the shuttle and dropped down again. "This is our maximum altitude and still in the wind shadow."

"Okay, hold our position here. Let's watch for the Thalgarin to show again. I think it will go in that hollow."

Their shuttle engines didn't make enough noise to be heard over the howl of the wind, so Tuatu parked' the craft and joined Ureth at the side window. They had a good view of the hollow in the mountain. Well, it was a little small to call it a mountain, but it probably was one at some time. There was a telltale round depression on the top, indicating it too had been volcanic at one point. The Thalgarin seemed to have picked a good place for a home.

They didn't wait too long before the Thalgarin came in view, pulling a sleek furred animal by the tail. It appeared to be dead, so it was clearly going to be a meal. It was when two tiny Thalgarins popped out of the hollow and greeted the big one, that Ureth and Tuatu realized it was a mom.

"Oh my, those cubs are adorable!" whispered Tuatu.

"You can't take one home."

Tuatu looked at him and saw his lips curve into a smile as he looked out the window. He wanted to take one home too.

The mother Thalgarin took the meal right up to the opening, and dropped it in the snow. Her cubs tore into the meat with a voraciousness that indicated their food supply was difficult to maintain. Their tiny squeaks were mixed with growls as they tore and ripped their way through their meal. When the young ones had their fill, their mom finished off the kill in a few bites.

There was virtually nothing left. Most of the bones had been eaten, along with the flesh and insides. Some telltale pieces were left behind, probably because they weren't healthy to eat. The mother Thalgarin picked up those pieces and carried them away from their hollow and buried them in the snow. Cleaning up kept their hollow safer from predators, but who would prey on one of these creatures?

"I'd love to get a look inside that hollow, but I don't want to disturb the young ones," said Ureth.

"Even though you want to capture one and bring it home?"

"Yes, even though. I suspect life here is hard enough not to make it even more so for the mother."

"So shall we cross over to the island then?"

"No, I would rather reach the end of the

peninsula."

"Then that's where we will head. VIRA, what is the direction to go?"

"The peninsula is actually not a solid piece of ground. In fact, my detailed scans done from space show that the curve of the peninsula is a chain of islands, all volcanic and they're connected by ice."

"Can we get there from here?"

"Oh yes, no problem. However, the further out we go, the worse the wind will get. There is a circumpolar ocean current that travels around the continent and there are no land masses to stop it. So it is very violent, windy, cold, and unpredictable. It moves the most water on the planet and is spinning westward."

"VIRA, what are the islands attached to?"

"They're attached to the seafloor, but it is considerably below sea level at this time. There are deep channels between the islands."

"VIRA, set a course for the peninsula please."

"Aye Captain."

Ureth and Tuatu were sitting in the flight deck and VIRA was flying the shuttle. As they flew over the snow and ice covered land, brown peaks appeared above the ice every now and then. They both watched the ground with binoculars to pick out details. Each of them kept a log of what they found, and the location. VIRA provided the location when they asked.

"Ahead is the peninsula."

Both of them put down their glasses and looked forward and saw a remarkable sight. Curving around the globe was a white crescent shaped arm stretching out into the deep ocean. Waves of unknown size were being pushed up to tall crests as the top of them was ripped away on the wind. The waves crashed into the shoreline that was predominantly rock, deep black. Some of the cliffs showed rock formed by layers and layers of different deposits, from sand to lava. The layers were twisted and folded on each other, demonstrating the power of tectonics to shape the land.

"This land was violently formed," said Ureth. "Look at those deformations!"

"There is volcanism there too. I've spotted more than one steaming cone," said Tuatu. "VIRA, can you get a temperature reading on the surface?"

"It appears that the temperature is 40 degrees below freezing point, but the wind is close to 3 Traverses per shard. That is extreme Captain. [This would be the equivalent of 3km/min or 180 km/hour.]"

"Can you try?"

"Yes, Captain." They felt the forward momentum of the shuttle stop and a gentle downward motion started, but that was quickly interrupted with swaying back and forth, rocking from side to side, and sudden drops like someone was pushing the craft to the ground. By the time VIRA set the shuttle down on the ground, Ureth looked a little green.

"Be careful when you exit. The ground is windswept, slippery, and you won't have much traction on the ground."

"Noted," said Tuatu. "Well, we better bundle up. This is not going to be pleasant."

Exiting the shuttle, Tuatu was hit by a wind force that nearly knocked her back inside the shuttle door. If it weren't for Ureth standing in the opening, the two of them would have ended up on the floor on their backs like turtles.

Pushing forward they doubled over to minimize the sting on their faces of ice crystals as they hit their faces. Ureth could hear tiny pings as the crystals hit his glasses and wondered for a moment if they would break under such bombardment.

Tuatu headed down the leeward side of the peak to try to get out of the wind. It lessened but was still howling around them. "This may not be a good place to explore today!" she yelled into the wind.

"Captain, you don't need to yell so loudly, I hear you!" said VIRA. "I can relay your words to the others without you needing to yell."

"Fine, please do. I can barely hear myself think with all this howling!"

Moments later, Ureth and Tuatu were both nodding agreement, so they returned to the shuttle. Just when they thought they had made it clear of injury, Ureth's foot slipped and dislodge a large block of ice. He lost his footing, and his knee crashed down, then his shoulder, and the next thing he knew, he was tumbling head over feet down the mountain

He screamed inside his helmet, and VIRA caught his words and relayed them to Tuatu, but it was a shard later than it happened, and they missed stopping him.

Tuatu watched as her friend slid and tumbled down the mountain, perhaps several Veylens before coming to a stop up against a large snow covered object. Ureth was face down and she could not determine if he was injured.

"His vital signs are elevated, but that must be from fear," said VIRA to Tuatu. "His breathing is very fast as is his heart rate. The blood pressure is nearly off the chart."

"Really? That would mean he is dead!" cried Tuatu.

"No, not really, sorry. I was exaggerating. He's banged up but fine. No fatal injuries detected. But we will have opportunities to tease him for slipping, right?"

"VIRA, if I didn't know better "

"Yes?"

"Never mind. How will we get him back?"

"I suggest we fly down there in the shuttle."

I need to get back inside the shuttle." Tuatu continued up the slope and braced herself when the full force of the wind hit her again. When she got back inside, she fell into the seating exhausted.

"I've never been so grateful for a ride in my life!" said Tuatu.

"You're welcome," said VIRA.

As Tuatu removed the bulkiest part of her environment suit, the breathing apparatus, the shuttle took off and was again bouncing in the wind. She felt it swoop up then down before it made a steady descent. The shuttle's engines slowed down until she felt the vehicle stop again.

"He's just outside the door," said VIRA.

The shuttle door opened, and there in front of them was a very large Thalgarin, sitting on the slope nearly covered completely with snow. Its eyes blinked and slowly focused on Tuatu's face. She could see its pupils open and close like the iris of a camera detecting light and adjusting focus. Finally they stopped and it was staring at her. Faint recognition shone on its face. The Thalgarin's jaw opened slightly and shut. It nodded and turned its head around to look at its back.

Ureth was just starting to stir when a clear single word screamed in his helmet: "STOP!" He froze in place in spite of the fact that he was face down and staring into snow. The screen of his mask protected his face from the biting snow. On the inside of the mask a vision formed, a Thalgarin. A big one. Sitting on top of him. Ureth grunted.

"Listen to me carefully, Ureth," whispered Tuatu from his ear piece. "You have come to rest against a Thalgarin. It's the one we saw before and she is very, very big. She just found out you're there and so far is doing nothing. But it's her butt you're up against. Do you copy?"

"Yes."

"Don't move!"

"No."

Tuatu hadn't broken visual contact with the Thalgarin. Being this close, she could look right at her at eye level. "You get around, don't you mama? Where are your cubs?" Tuatu asked the Thalgarin.

The creature looked at Tuatu for a moment then made a noise like nothing she had ever heard before. It was something between a laugh, a snort, and a yawn.

The Thalgarin blinked again, slower this time. A low, layered hum rose in her throat not a growl, not a warning. It was curious. She shifted her weight slightly, lifting one massive paw and lowering it with delicate precision until it rested gently almost reverently on Ureth's helmet. A sound like softened snow compressing echoed inside.

Tuatu inhaled sharply, but the paw remained still.

Then the creature turned her head toward the shuttle not toward Tuatu, but toward the embedded speaker port. VIRA's optical sensor glowed faintly there, a quiet observer.

The Thalgarin made a second sound shorter, higher-pitched, almost questioning. Then she looked back at Tuatu, blinking. Her head tilted, just slightly.

"Captain," VIRA said softly, "I believe she just asked you something."

Tuatu stepped forward, instinct overriding logic. "Is he is he mine?" she asked aloud, unsure if the creature would understand, but needing to respond.

The Thalgarin lowered her head and gave a short, amused snort steam curling from her nostrils. She withdrew her paw, then reached it out again this time, toward Tuatu.

Not aggressively. Just open. Waiting.

Tuatu didn't move.

The creature's massive claws sank into the snow

beside her and, with surprising grace, she drew a single slow spiral. Then she stood, snow shedding from her fur in glittering veils, and vanished into the wind.

Ureth scrambled out of the snow and launched himself into the shuttle. Laying in a heap of snow and limbs, Tuatu bent down and helped him extricate himself from the equipment.

"Captain," VIRA said after a pause, "I recorded the vocal patterns. There were resonances similar to my own. I think she thought Ureth was your cub?"

A strangled noise came from Ureth..

Tuatu didn't miss a beat. "Don't push your luck."

They stood in silence for a long moment, staring out into the swirling snow.

"Captain," VIRA said, "Shall I initiate our crossing?"

Tuatu turned toward the shuttle, her hand brushing the spiral the Thalgarin had etched. "Yes," she said softly. "Let's cross."

The shuttle lifted, nosing into the harsh wind, heading out across the open waters between the peninsula and the faint, mist-wrapped silhouette of the South American continent. Waves below churned in deep rhythm, and icebergs floated like sleeping titans in the sea.

Tuatu took her seat beside Ureth. "Let's see what kind of old gods sleep on this side."

Chapter 18
Ruins of Older Gods

[SILENCE — CYCLE 10]

The shuttle rose into the wind and carried them in a long, slow arc over the open water. Below, floes of ice churned between waves, trailing white scars across the black sea. VIRA remained mostly silent, only occasionally noting turbulence or adjusting flight path to avoid aerial downdrafts.

The first sight of land was a low ridge rising like a brow from the surf. It was dark, jagged, but high. It had long ridges of mountains arranged in north-south lines. The mountains were rugged, tall and ice capped, but the valleys were lined with trees and grasslands. There was flowing fresh water here.

The mountains they had been following seemed to continue up the western edge of this land mass like a spine protecting the eastern softer parts of the continent.

They traced the curve of a river inland until they found a place to land: a shelf high above the sea, shielded on three sides by wind-smoothed stone. The shuttle touched down in silence.

Ureth was the first to step outside. He stood for a long moment, visor angled upward.

Tuatu followed. "What do you see?"

"Terracing," he said quietly. "Natural, at first glance but too regular. Too intentional."

Tuatu narrowed her eyes. The pattern was unmistakable. Flat steps carved into the rock, not for erosion control, but for placement. Settlement.

"VIRA," she said. "Can you scan for regular geometries?"

"I already have. There are right angles embedded in the cliffside. At least six concentric levels. Elevation-based. Patterned."

"Structures?" Ureth asked.

"Ruins," VIRA confirmed. "Long buried. Not modern. Not ours."

"Could they be from the bipeds?" Tuatu asked.

VIRA paused.

"Negative. The wear patterns and substructure placement suggest construction at least twenty thousand

Earth years ago. Possibly more."

Tuatu exchanged a look with Ureth. She stepped closer to the edge, brushing snow from a flat black slab of stone. Faint lines almost erased ran beneath the ice. Spiral, radial, intersecting.

Not Zydean. Not human. "Older Gods indeed," she whispered, "Then they came before."

"This is truly a magical place," said VIRA, floating up beside the captain where she was looking out over the valley below them. "It makes sense that someone would have built a city here."

"Indeed it is. The air is thinner up here, but the ozone is stimulating and it smells so sweet."

Looking around they were alone on top of the mountain with the ruins. The grass waved in the wind that blew up the slopes.

"Why don't we stay here a while?" asked Ureth. "Perhaps we could build ourselves an outpost here. It's easily accessible for the pod, we could put the landing pad over there," he pointed to one peak. "And we could build some sleeping quarters and facilities for preparing whatever we hunt on this spot."

"Like an away tent?" she nodded. "I can see that."

"Well, I brought something a bit more durable than a tent. It's a portable dome."

"We could set up on the terraces that already exist here," said Tuatu. She walked over to the first terrace. Look how rigorously the vegetation grows. It must be good quality soil. Yes, let's build an away camp. Maybe even a more permanent one."

"We shall make arrangements for more permanent structures when we get back to the city," said Ureth.

"Wendell can help you with crew and supplies. We'll stay here tonight and then return in the morning. VIRA, put the pod into Station Staying mode."

"Right away Captain," said VIRA.

"Where shall we set up camp?" asked Tuatu.

"Over there, it's nice and flat. I'll get the dome," said Ureth.

In her mind's eye Tuatu was seeing the city he described. It would take them a few cycles to build it out, and until then they could live in temporary shelters, but it would be spectacular.

"I can see it," said Tuatu. "That hill over there, just to the left of the dragon back cliffs, could be the government house."

"Dragon back?" asked Ureth.

"Sorry, my imagination," said Tuatu. "See that tallest peak with the ridge line extending behind it? It looks like a dragon's back to me."

"Oh I see it!" said Ureth. "Those two smaller bumps in front could be the neck and head. And now I see the hill you mean for the government house. Yes, that would be perfect."

The two of them stood quiet for a few Shards looking at the beauty of the mountains, each seeing a vision of the city they would build.

"You were right, those domes really do pop up!" said Tuatu just a Prism later, when all the temporary structures were erected; a private sleeping area for each of them with a chemical toilet in each; and a place to eat in case they got weather. VIRA helped by stringing some lights from one to the other encircling the small camp in a bath of warm light.

"I didn't know you had such lights, VIRA," said Tuatu.

"Made them up from some lights inside the shuttle. They were already strips of lights, I was just able to lengthen them."

"Very creative. And it adds a nice homey feel."

"Thank you for noticing."

Ureth came walking back up the mountain from going for a walk. He was holding something in his hand. "I've brought supper!"

"What is that?" asked Tuatu.

"They appear to be small mammals, and they're vegetarian, so I figured we can probably eat them."

"And just how do we eat them?"

"I can instruct you," said VIRA. There are plenty of cooking instructions in my archive."

"I will set a fire in the meantime and prepare a cooking platform." Ureth started looking for material suitable for burning and picked up some small dead brush, sticks, and eventually a dead tree.

"Where did you learn to do this?" asked Tuatu. She returned with the furry little creatures skinned, and set on a spit to roast over the fire.

"Oh I learned this a long, long time ago from my grandfather's stories. He told of traditions where the young men would go out in the wilds and have to survive on what they could catch and eat. I was an avid student and paid close attention to the parts about making fire. It's a simple process really. You need flammable material, a spark, and oxygen. The small twigs burn nicely but quickly which is why I also have larger wood."

"And how will you make a spark?"

"Well, I'll use our technology for that," he said, grinning.

It wasn't long before he had a sizable fire burning in the small circle of stones he laid first.

"And what are the stones for?"

"To prevent the fire from spreading. That would be a problem."

"I'll get the Virellan and some glasses," said Tuatu, heading back to the shuttle. She walked into a conversation between VIRA and Wendell. It sounded like they were talking about cooking, but there was innuendo mixed in there too.

"What are you two talking about?" she asked.

"You and Ureth of course," said VIRA. "Both Wendell and I have noticed a growing intimacy between you two. Are you a couple yet?"

"Wendell, did you want me or Ureth for something?" asked Tuatu.

"Sorry, Captain. It's just that there may be a problem brewing here at home."

"We were returning in the morning. Can it wait?"

"Yes, I believe it can, Captain."

"Then we'll see you tomorrow, Wendell."

"Have a romantic evening, Captain," said Wendell. Then the radio went silent. Tuatu made a small noise in her throat and exited the shuttle with the glasses and wine.

VIRA made a note of the exchange in her personal

log.

It was a remarkable sunset on top of the mountain, but as the sun got closer to the horizon, it got colder outside. Out in front of the shelter was a small wood fire letting off a wondrous scent and he noticed a fair amount of heat. He looked around the campe and was satisfied that it was a touch romantic and comfortable. He didn't know where this would go, but he wanted to keep doors open.

When he spotted the Captain exiting the pod, he was pleased to see she had chosen to change from her flight suit into casual clothes. She was carrying the two glasses and a bottle he recognized. He wanted to get to know this woman.

"This looks lovely, Ureth," she said. She walked right up to the fire, sat down on one of the seats' he had provided, and placed the glasses and bottle on the ground. Rubbing her hands near the fire, she felt herself relax. "I'm glad you thought of a shelter, because I think it is going to be cold up here after sundown."

"So do I. You look breathtaking in the sunset light. And don't worry, I have heaters inside the domes as well as some thick blankets and pillows on which to sit."

"Thank you Ureth, but we won't need two, will we?" She poured out the Virellan and handed him a glass. The two of them sipped the beverage, remembering back to the first evening they were together like this and how potent the wine had been.

"Do you want to stay here by the fire or go inside?" asked Ureth.

"Let's sit by the fire until we cannot."

VIRA Log

[SILENCE 35 — CYCLE 10]

It would seem my Captain and Ureth are growing closer. Will this change their working relationship?

End log.

234

Chapter 19
The Breaking

[SILENCE 35 — SPIRAL 15, CYCLE 15]

The Grand Dome no longer echoed like it once had. Time had filled it with voices, children, layered repairs, and the warmth of routine. But tonight, the chamber stood quiet and shadowed, lit only by the spiral lamps set into the walls amber against stone. Tuatu and Ureth sat together near the central dais, reviewing reports of recent glacier shifts in the east when the doors opened.

Sern Valat, Elder Continuant, stepped through.

He moved like he carried something ancient on his back not his age, but expectation, weightier with each Silence. His outer coat bore the silver stripes of those who still considered themselves of the ship, not of the soil. The Continuants kept their distinction carefully, quietly, and without compromise.

Ureth stood to greet him. "Elder Valat. You come late."

Valat's nod was measured. "Time has passed. And still there is no reply."

Tuatu's eyes narrowed slightly. "We send messages every Spiral. The array functions. But Zydee does not answer."

"Zydee must answer," Valat replied, his voice rising not in anger, but grief. "We lit the beacon the day we landed. We maintained the protocols. We preserved the Ship's core ethics, its authority. We remembered."

He stepped forward. "And yet six thousand Silences. No call. No acknowledgment. Nothing."

Tuatu glanced at Ureth. He inclined his head a silent signal: let him speak.

Tuatu rose. "We were prepared for silence, Sern. We hoped for more, but we prepared."

"I was not," Valat said. "Nor were those who remain with me. We preserved the Arvidan because one day, it would rise again. Not to abandon it. Not to bury it in ice and memory. The colony thrives because we protect its spine."

"And now?" Ureth asked. "What are you seeking from us?"

Sern looked at the two of them for a long moment,

the silence so complete that the flickering of the spiral lamps seemed to pulse in rhythm with their hearts.

"We seek closure," he said softly. "If Zydee will not answer us then we must seek answers ourselves."

Tuatu's brow furrowed. "You want to leave."

Valat nodded. "Six shuttles remain docked to the Arvidan. Our Continuants are ready. We wish to break orbit. Search out the other colonies. Confirm their fates. We would take the Arvidan its heart is still strong. But its soul is Earthbound now. So we will not ask."

Ureth stepped forward. "Then what do you ask?"

"Sanction. Recognition of our departure. And a promise that we will be remembered, should we not return."

Tuatu looked at him long and deeply. "You will be remembered. Always."

Sern bowed slightly, the motion formal and ancient. "Then we leave at Spiral's end."

As he turned to go, Tuatu called after him. "Sern if you find them if you find Zydee what will you tell them of us?"

He paused at the threshold. His reply came like a whisper etched in stone.

"That you listened to the Earth. That you rooted.

That you became."

And then he was gone.

It began with raised voices in the hydroponic commons.

Dozens of colonists had gathered for shift-cycle rations when someone shouted across the hall.

"You just want to keep the Ark ship to yourselves!"

The speaker a thin-faced engineer named Korien jabbed a finger toward a cluster of Continuants, identifiable by their still-immaculate uniforms and braided data sashes.

"You people don't grow food. You don't help with mining. You barely touch the ground "

A Continuant, voice smooth but cold, replied, "We maintain mission integrity. You wouldn't be breathing without the ship."

"Then maybe you should come live on the planet, like the rest of us," growled a farmer named Dareth. "Instead of playing gods in orbit."

Pushing. Shouting. Someone threw a nutrient packet. Another shoved a shoulder too hard.

Then fists.

It escalated fast two colonists tackled a Continuant to the floor while others tried to pull them apart. Furniture crashed. Children screamed.

The hallway lights flashed amber a security alert.

Then, VIRA's voice cut across the station:

"Attention all personnel. A long-range message has been received. Please report to Grand Dome for interpretation and coordination."

The crowd froze.

One Continuant stood, blood on his cheek, and locked eyes with Korien.

"This changes nothing," he said quietly.

Korien spat, but said nothing. The crowd began to disperse, slowly some in awe, others in suspicion.

Tuatu and Ureth had already been running toward the hall. They arrived just as the last of the scuffle was fading. Tuatu swept her gaze across the crowd, stopping briefly on the injured.

"Secure this area," she told a security aide. "No arrests yet. No punishments. Not until we understand what that message is."

Ureth touched her shoulder, his voice low. "If it's real this time "

"It won't matter," she murmured. "They've already begun to split."

The Grand Dome filled with colonists faster than it had in many Spirals. The news of a received message had spread like a pulse through the colony quick, electric, full of possibility.

Tuatu stood beside Ureth on the upper dais, both in formal grey. Neither had spoken yet.

Below them, thousands waited some hopeful, some with clenched jaws and tight shoulders. A small group of Continuants stood near the front, eyes fixed on the projection wall with rigid anticipation.

VIRA's voice filled the space.

"The following data burst was received via long-range subspace transband. Duration: 4.2 shards. Origin unknown. Language partially scrambled. Processing now."

A ripple of murmurs rose and fell. Tuatu stepped forward.

"This may be the first signal we've received since Silence 1. Remain calm. VIRA play it."

The screen flared with static. Then a voice broke through garbled, alien, layered with distortion.

" Arvidan coordinate failure anomaly spreading hold not safe "

More static. Then a sharp ping a code signature.

"Signature match confirmed. This originates from the vessel Hariven Dawn, last recorded location: Rimward Spiral Sector. Mission: Resource World Survey, Zydee Protocol Chain A-7."

A stunned silence followed.

Ureth exhaled slowly. "One of ours."

But Tuatu's brow furrowed. "It's not a call to rendezvous."

VIRA's voice returned.

"Message reconstruction: 62% complete. Contextual analysis suggests: warning or distress call. Key phrases: containment breach,' planetfall unsuccessful,' anomaly unknown.'"

Gasps broke out across the dome.

"What does it mean?" someone shouted. "Are they still alive?"

"Is Zydee gone?"

A Continuant stepped forward. Sern Valat. His voice was level, but urgent.

"If the Hariven Dawn failed we may be the only viable colony. We must preserve what remains."

Tuatu lifted her hand, silencing the room. "We don't know yet. We'll investigate this fully. But until we do stay focused. We have one world. One future. Let's not tear it apart."

She looked to Ureth. He met her eyes and nodded once.

Later, alone in a side corridor, Tuatu whispered, "It wasn't what they wanted."

"No," Ureth said. "But it might be what they needed."

The hangar was dim power rerouted for engine calibration. Sparks flared from open panels beneath the hull of Shuttle 17, the modified long-range craft that had become the focus of quiet obsession for a certain subset of Continuants.

When Tuatu arrived, she was already running.

"Seal the outer doors," she barked into her comm. "Disable the launch track. Quietly."

From the catwalk above, she looked down at a half-dozen figures moving urgently around the shuttle loading final supplies, checking alignment, running their own diagnostic overrides.

Ureth caught up to her, breathless. "They're not waiting."

"They heard the message," she said grimly. "Now they're running."

Four members of the Enclosure Arieveth's

peacekeeping corps filed in behind her. Not soldiers. Not anymore. But trained.

Tuatu descended the steps fast, boots hitting the floor with the weight of command.

"Sern Valat!" she shouted.

Silence fell instantly.

He emerged from the shadows of the loading bay, hands raised but not ashamed. "We were going to tell you. After."

Tuatu stepped forward, eyes narrowed. "You were going to take the shuttle, unannounced, and jump into a storm of distortion and unknown dangers. Without our agreement."

Valat's voice remained calm. "You saw the message. Zydee may be gone. The legacy of our civilization "

"Will not survive on a stolen shuttle!" she snapped. "We had an agreement."

The others around him froze.

Ureth stepped forward now. "You want to leave? Fine. But not like this."

Tuatu nodded. "Sern Valat came to us three Spirals ago. He asked for an accord permission to take the Arvidan and six shuttles. Not out of betrayal. Out of purpose."

She swept the room with her eyes. "We debated. We argued. But in the end we agreed."

Gasps rippled. Several of the Continuants turned sharply to stare at Valat.

"You were to leave for the ceremony. With records. With witnesses. With blessing. Not as thieves."

Valat lowered his hands. His voice softened. "I was afraid... the longer we waited, the more we would oppose it."

Tuatu's voice dropped, but it cut like wind over ice. "So you decided to flee in the dark."

She turned to the Enclosure. "Stand down. No arrests. No charges."

Then to the gathered Continuants. "You'll leave in four Spirals. On our terms. With honor. Or not at all."

Valat hesitated then bowed. "Agreed."

Tuatu exhaled, tension unwinding. She looked up at the ancient ribs of the Arvidan looming high above. Her voice was quiet now, meant only for Ureth:

"I never thought I'd give her up."

"She was only ever meant to carry us here," Ureth replied. "Now she carries something else."

The day had come.

High above Arieveth's central plaza, the cliff-side platforms bloomed open like stone petals. For generations, they had remained sealed, hidden behind the mountain's ridges. Now, with the ice melted back by heat-vents and reinforced supports humming quietly, six launch ramps extended into the air, awaiting their vessels. The Ark ship loomed behind, its great bulk humming with life sleek, scarred, and still magnificent.

Every colonist had gathered. Thousands filled the dome and overflowed into the lower terraces, dressed in formal weaves dyed in the blues and silvers of departure. It was not a farewell of triumph, nor of exile but of divergence. Of possibility.

Tuatu stood at the edge of the platform, clad in her Command robes, the glyph for Silence embroidered in spiral-thread at her throat. Beside her, Ureth held the sealed list of names the 310 Continuants who would leave, and the six pilots who would guide the shuttles through unknown skies.

A hush fell across the crowd.

Sern Valat stepped forward. The Continuants' leader had aged in the past few Silences, his once-severe voice now holding the weathered depth of conviction. He bowed to Tuatu, then faced the people.

"We were not made to remain still," he said.

"Some among us were born for the Spiral of Departure. We remember Zydee's sky not just as a memory, but as a mandate. We are Continuants. We will not give up the search."

The crowd remained still not cold, not angry. Just... reverent. They had debated, resisted, mourned and finally, understood.

Tuatu took one step forward. "You leave with our blessing. And with our sorrow. You carry the dream of Zydee, and of us. We ask only that you send word, should you find something new. Or should you need to return."

Sern nodded. "We will."

Then came the ritual. The youngest children stepped forward from the crowd children born on Earth, the First Root generation. Each held a crystal coil of polished spiral-glass, woven with shimmering strands of memory-data and starlight. One by one, they offered them to the departing Continuants.

"For remembrance," whispered one child.

"For our story," said another.

"For what comes next," whispered a third.

The Continuants bowed low. Some wept. Others stood with the stillness of purpose.

The platform pulsed once in deep gold. The boarding began.

Six shuttles hissed open, their ramps kissing the stone. One by one, the Continuants filed inside. Sern was the last to board. He turned, placed his hand over his heart, and spoke only once more.

"Spiral strong. Silence deep. We will find a path."

Tuatu raised her hand, palm outward, and the crowd followed. The parting spiral.

The ships lifted in perfect synchrony. Engines hummed. Light flared. Snow caught in their wakes like stars torn loose from gravity.

They vanished into the sky, arcing toward the horizon.

Silence fell again not heavy, but full.

The people did not move.

Finally, Ureth spoke. "They go not as deserters. But as seekers."

Tuatu nodded. "And we remain. As roots."

Far above, the sky wheeled on. Beneath the ice, the Spiral turned.

Chapter 20
The Stillness After

[SILENCE 37]

The Grand Assembly Hall hummed with low conversation. It wasn't often that all the House Elders, scientific leads, logistics teams, and citizen delegates were called together. The room carved into the mountain's inner vault had been expanded three times since Silence 20. Its domed ceiling reflected simulated star fields, while the surrounding walls displayed moving data: resource inventories, thermal scans of the volcano's inner core, long-range sub-ice topography.

At the center stood Tuatu and Ureth, flanked by Sern Valat's former second-in-command, now repurposed as the liaison between Arieveth and the newly departed Continuants.

Tuatu opened the meeting with a gesture both hands rising, then sweeping down to rest over her heart.

"Thank you for coming," she said, her voice steady, amplified by the subtle soundweb embedded in the dome. "As of this morning, the Ark ship Arvidan and the Continuants have left. Six of the forty shuttles have gone with them. We have confirmed their departure vector, and we've agreed to continue subspace communication... though as of now, the channels are empty."

The murmurs quieted. She continued, "Now it is time to face our own future. Arieveth is thriving but crowded. Resources are stable, but not infinite. And above us is an entire planet we have not touched."

Ureth stepped forward, activating the wall display. A rotating, slowly revealed map of the planet shimmered into view. "Based on long-range atmospheric and geological scans, we believe there are at least four temperate zones, three major freshwater systems, and a dozen tectonic shelters that could serve as future settlements." The map pulsed, highlighting areas of interest. "But these are just theories. We need real data. We need to explore."

A voice from the Agricultural House rose from the side. "And if the new regions are uninhabitable? If we scatter ourselves and cannot regroup?"

"That is why we're not scattering aimlessly," Tuatu replied. "We will send thirty-two of the remaining thirty-four shuttles each with a carefully selected crew of scientists, builders, scouts, and communicators. Each team will be autonomous for one Silence. After that, they will either return, report, or request expansion."

Another Elder stood, arms folded. "And who decides who goes?"

"We do," said Ureth. "Together. Every House will nominate candidates. Each team must have cross-disciplinary strength engineering, biology, diplomacy, survival. No mission is without risk. But each is an opportunity to seed the Spiral in new soil."

Someone called out from the back, "Why now?"

Tuatu didn't hesitate. "Because we are not meant to huddle forever in stone. Zydee was dying. Arieveth is thriving. But Earth is living. We must learn how to live with it not just within it."

A long silence followed.

Then one by one, voices began to rise not in dissent, but in contribution. Suggestions. Volunteers. Tactical concerns. Naming protocols. Data relay structures. It was a chorus of resolve, uncertainty, and purpose what Zydeans might call the First Spiral of Becoming.

By the meeting's end, the Council had been formed of all the leaders of the different houses. There were 35 council members.

"I have one other resolution to put forth," said the

leader of one of the groups. "We elect Tuatu and Ureth to be our chieftains." There was a lot of agreement and the resolution passed easily.

"We hereby award you the title Commander, Ureth, and Tuatu, will retain her title Captain."

The entire population clapped in approval of this nomination, as Ureth, now Commander, and Tuatu stood and accepted the honor.

The Spiral would widen.

Thirty-two shuttles. Thirty-two new paths. Captain Tuatu will have one of them. Her team was to travel as far as the ice in the north and see what they could find.

And beneath it all, the hum of the planet waiting.

VIRA Log

[SILENCE 37 — SPIRAL 6, CYCLE 18]

Ark ship Arvidan Internal Systems Access Code [VIRA-DELTA-7]

Population within Arieveth has reached an optimal density threshold.

We have been on Arvidan for 37 Silences or 7,400

Earth solar cycles.

Exploration by the 32 Teams has found many ideal locations for a new city for our people. The mapping of each location has taken many earth-cycles, as well the documenting of flora and fauna.

Life-support systems in Arieveth are functioning at 93.2% projected long-term capacity.

No signal returns from Ark ships Halenet, Moravai, or Zeltrin despite 22 Silences of attempted contact.

Internal consensus divergence detected. Continuant protocol requests activated.

Recommendation: bifurcation of settlement initiative for long-term planetary viability.

Note: Captain Tuatu and Commander Ureth Sortain leadership has stabilized the population.

Subtextual alert: decision points loom.

End log.

"We have been on this planet for 42 Silences. If we counted the number of solar years, that would be 8,400 Earth years. That seems like such a high number for the time we have been here. But the rhythms of this planet are different even though we've kept the light rhythms of our homeworld in our city.

Our city grows, now that the ship is no longer in the cave, we have been able to use that space as well. We have harnessed the geothermal power of this mountain and built power plants to provide us with everything we need. While the underground capacity is vast, we will eventually need more room.

Receiving that signal has shown me that we have become safe in our world. We have not been monitoring what is happening on the surface and thus unaware of what is happening. It's time we get out of our mountain, and explore the world we have decided to live on.

Our medical center is busy with new births. The new children born here are slightly different from those who came here. Their physique is different. They are taller, stronger, and their senses are more sharp than ours.

The doctors have explained this to me, that the gravity being a bit less than our home world has let them grow taller. With this population steadily growing we are near overcrowded. We need to find more local food.

The local population of Oorithi have become friends, so we couldn't think of turning them into food. We get too much enjoyment out of watching them play, and interacting with them.

I am much disturbed by the fact that I have yet to

hear anything back from any of the other ships. But VIRA's Whisperspan has made contact with something, and it appears whatever it is now, it was our ark ship that the Continuants took to leave for their own journey.

The light in Arieveth's hydrodomes was timed to simulate a natural Zydean dawn. Rows of leafy greens glistened beneath dew emitters as the nutrient mists were turned on for the day. Children ran barefoot through the low corridors, their laughter echoing between the vertical gardens. An older Zydean named Kelri was instructing a group of children in how to prune their rootfronds without damaging the cluster.

"Every Spiral, every Aven of root you tend this is our breath," she reminded them. One boy nodded solemnly, cradling a tiny bundle of leaflings like treasure.

He plunged his hand into the soil and made a small crater before dropping the plant into it. Lovingly he covered the roots and pressed down before watering the plant a few drops. He picked up the basket of seedlings and moved down the row to plant another.

Meanwhile, a young girl was doing the same thing on another row, just like all the children in that class. Together about 30 children were sowing the new generation of plants to be harvested.

This community effort sustained them. They had created huge planting mezzanines inside the crater where the natural light filters in more intensely. The top of the crater was sealed off with a transparent dome, letting in the maximum amount of light. The crater interior was kept warm with heat lamps powered by geothermal energy. The ice melted inside the crater very slowly, and that provided them with water.

In repair bay two, two young engineers, Roen and Vistra, were adjusting the power grid interfaces to balance the load, when VIRA's voice chirped in through a wall panel.

"Warning: if you cross those wires again, I'll be forced to file a misconduct report to your ancestors."

One of the technicians, Roen grinned and said, "She's getting sarcastic again."

"Oh, sweet Roen. That wasn't sarcasm. That was love."

The panel flickered, then played a brief snippet of a Zydean opera before resuming normal output. Vistra blinked and made a sidelong glance at Roen, then shook his head.

"You do have strange girlfriends, Roen," he said.

"Well, at least I have a girlfriend."

In the converted lava tunnel, the Zydeans had set up a market. Every day, they would bring things to trade, such as woven fiber, fermented vinefruit, hand-fashioned instruments, and containers of preserved leaf-sap. The old barter system was alive and well. It had served them well before and they saw no reason to change the system.

Tuatu walked through quietly, smiling when she wasn't recognized, observing the citizens in their everyday rhythms. She paused at a stall where a child had painted glyphs on stone and arranged them in spiral patterns.

"Do these mean anything yet?" she asked.

The child beamed. "They mean what you want them to."

"Then I shall say they mean life." The little girl's smile widened even more.

Tuatu made it back to the large cave that had been carved into the heart of the mountain. Inside the cave was a large table carved out of the rock from the ground up. It was large enough to seat 40 people. She and Ureth had been using it as a meeting room, but they figured it would be a good council chamber. Ureth was waiting for her.

Ureth stood beside the beautifully carved table that had chairs set around it. Standing and looking awkward were some of the Elders of the population and some others. These folks represented the people and came from all professions: engineers, medics, a teacher, and even one cook.

Ureth addressed the assembled people, "My friends, we have come here and made a home. We grow, we thrive, and we continue. However, we cannot stay hidden in this place. We will eventually become too numerous to live here comfortably. Therefore the next step must be taken. "We must begin the Age of the Root. And we must decide where to grow."

There was a murmur of voices as people in the assemblage agreed.

"I invite you to take a seat here in this chamber as a member of our new Council," said Tuatu.

"Will you be on our Council, Tuatu?" asked one of the Elders.

"I will if you would like me to be."

"I think it's generally unanimous that both you and Ureth should lead this Council. After all, you have been our de facto leaders for 38 Silences," said another Elder.

Ureth acknowledge the invitation for both of them, and everyone took their seats.

A heated discussion followed about allocating more geothermal vents, whether to send another scouting team west, and how to handle the increasing population density.

Neither Tuatu nor Ureth took part in the discussion until they were asked.

"Our leaders have been notably quiet during this discussion. What say you?" asked an Elder.

"We've seen the breadth of this land," said Tuatu. "And what we haven't seen our shuttles will. We're not here to rule we're here to guide."

"We need to set up exploration missions and send them to different locations on this planet. Tuatu, can you organize this?"

"Yes, I can. I will happily lead one of those missions myself."

"As I will accompany the Captain," said Ureth.

In a dim corridor overlooking the ice, VIRA's voice spoke to herself, soft, unmonitored."They speak of roots and families, laughter and fear. I was built to calculate... but I think I am beginning to feel the shape of this world."

Her presence shimmered briefly in the polished wall an abstract reflection, not quite humanoid yet. But almost. So very close.

Later that same evening, in the quiet of a diagnostics chamber VIRA had commandeered for herself, VIRA assembled a frame.

It was not fully Zydean, nor fully human. A hybrid shell of silvery polyalloy and translucent flexbone. Graceful and slender, shaped by her observations of those she served. In the chamber mirror, a soft face took shape minimal, unfinished, but with unmistakable eyes: luminous, curious, rimmed in silver.

"They gave me form in code," she said softly to herself. "But now... I give myself form in matter."

On the wall beside her, her own spiral glyph appeared a signature made by her own calculations. It glowed faintly, like the first ember of a soul taking root.

Chapter 21
Charting Tomorrow

[SILENCE 43 — CYCLE 10]

The Day of the First Root had passed long into song and memory, but its echoes still danced in the halls of Arieveth. Every year now, there was a Name Day, where the same celebration happened. The population was growing quickly, their laughter pushing at the ship's edges, their dreams straining against old walls.

The Continuants had also been given their choice and set free to explore further in the universe. May their voyage sing through the stars.

It was time.

Since the council meeting of 37, plans were downsized and simplified. Ten teams went out initially, scoping out general areas first. From their earliest scans of the planet from outer space, they had targeted several landing points for their shuttlecraft. They needed to make sure those locations would not be compromised by the people living there.

Each crew will be responsible for searching the immediate area for a spot suitable to build on, taking inventory of minerals, flora, and fauna in the area, determining where or if humans are close by (which would eliminate that location), and doing a geological survey of the area.

Tuatu stood before the exploration council, a circle of engineers, scholars, and envoys gathered around a shifting map of the land beyond the crater.

VIRA's voice guided them, weaving data streams into living topography.

"Preliminary scans indicate viable flora and fauna within a five-Luneth radius. Stable geothermal vents, freshwater sources, and migratory patterns suggest seasonal abundance."

The projected landscape shifted with layers of information. The ice-crusted plains gave way to valleys where volcanic warmth bled upward, allowing mosses and hardy grasses to survive. Patches of stunted willow-like shrubs and creeping vines clung to rocky outcrops.

The image shifted and on the screen was a different land, with tall trees of a different type, that had long fronds all connected at the very top. The trunks were often curved and the fronds looked like pom-poms on the end of a stick. Some of these trees had large fruit hanging from the top as well. That land had different creatures running around, and was flush with flowers and birds.

The image shifted again to a vast sea of sand shifting in the wind. The waves looked just like the waves on the sea, but they were stationary. Dotting the sand were small specs of green with more of those pom-pom trees. Mountains edged the sand seas, and appeared to be ancient rock.

Yet again the image blurred and moved to another location. This one was close to ice. Vast plains of grass with large land animals roaming over it. Huge beasts with great horns. Humans were following them. Their backdrop was an enormous cliff of ice that framed the whole land, which was woven with streams of water from the glaciers and dotted with vast lakes.

"Teams," Tuatu started. "These are some of the vistas you will find where you go. This planet is varied greatly in its composition, climate, and geology. Humans are not everywhere, so there is still plenty of territory for us. We seek a new location to build a satellite city. One that will give us room to grow our population, as well as start to grow some native crops. We need to start adapting to this planet."

"Up to now we have kept our own timekeeping, our own sense of the Silence. But from now on, we shall move to the rhythms of this planet. Time will move faster because their planet is smaller and their solar system is also smaller. A Silence here is but a fraction of ours. Their Spirals are indeed shorter too. But you will adapt."

"You will also notice that your bodies will feel stronger, your senses will appear sharper. This is a gift from the Spiral to us. On this world, because we are accustomed to much harsher environments, this one will feel easy. Our sharper hearing was useful to pick out noises in a very noisy world, but here it is quiet. Our strength was needed to overcome heavier gravity, but here it lets us do more."

"I warn you to be careful though. Do not let humans see you, or see the differences between us. We don't know much about them yet. Something we have to rectify, and quickly. Tomorrow you will all set out with a one cycle mission. You can monitor their time by watching the moon. Tomorrow it will be at it's fullest point. Call that Full Moon. You have until the moon is at its fullest again. That is about 29 revolutions of the planet. Mark the beginning of the daylight. That will be called the beginning of one revolution or one day. We will refine this timekeeping system over the next few Cycles."

"Good luck to all, and don't forget to submit a report every Spiral. VIRA will be keeping a log, and compiling the results for us. Good night, and may the Spiral turn in your favour!"

The following morning Tuatu arrived at her shuttlepod at the crack of the Zydean Spiral. She had no idea when it was outside, but they'll all find out soon enough. Her morning beverage was steaming in her hand as she inhaled its aroma blissfully while leaning against the side of her craft.

"Good morning Thiopeta," said a familiar and welcome voice.

Opening one eye judiciously, Tuatua squinted at Ureth. "Is it a good morning or is my beverage lulling me into a blissful state?"

"Shouldn't it be waking you up?" he chuckled low as he came up beside her. Gently brushing a strand of hair behind her ear, he planted a delicate kiss on her cheek.

"Mmm," Tuatu smiled. "That was nice." She opened both her eyes and looked straight into his handsome face. She hadn't really looked at him before, but she did now. The gentle lines around his eyes that showed he liked to smile, the curve of his jaw indicating strength, and thick head of hair drifting down to his shoulders and back indicating a major bloodline. He was a handsome man.

They have been enjoying each other's company for a few Silences now. They were comfortable in each other's space and bodies. Their joining was inevitable after that first intense night, but she still hadn't expected the bond. Being bonded to Ureth had become something very special; they could feel each other's heart, read each other's emotions, and often thought as one. They had one rule though, to act professionally in public, in spite of who they were in private.

This kiss almost broke that rule, except there wasn't anyone else around yet. "You're lucky no one is here and we're alone!" teased Tuatu.

"Oh? Would you have disciplined me?" he asked. The mirth was clearly visible on his face as he struggled to keep it straight. "Pity, I would have enjoyed that."

Tuatu pelted him with harmless punches to his shoulder until she heard someone clearing their throat behind her. Turning around, she saw Wendell standing there, pack in hand and smiling.

"I see I've been assigned with your team again? Was that a coincidence?" he asked.

"Not in the slightest," said Tuatu. "We'll wait for the rest of our group. That will be Nevril, T'shaya, VIRA, Halen, and Mivva. We have a few others joining us as well." At that moment, three of the team members approached speaking animatedly amongst themselves. They nodded at Wendell, Tuatu, and Ureth before entering the shuttle and stowing their gear and finding a seat.

As soon as the last of their team was aboard, Wendell got clearance to leave. As always, the ascent out of the crater took Ureth's breath away. Not only was the transition from their crater city to the surface of ice dramatic and beautiful, but she always forgot just how bright the star of this system was. It was blinding.

"Ack! Someone, hand me a pair of light shades for my eyes!!!" Ureth passed out the vision-saving shades that one of their engineers had invented from a polymer he extracted out of an oily substance. The shades created a barrier of color between the eye and the star deep enough that you weren't impaired. It was like standing in the shade of a dense tree or building with a canopy overhead. They fit neatly on one's head gear with a strap around the back of the head.

Shades in place, Tuatu and the others were face planted to their windows looking at everything. Many had not yet been outside of their crater so it was all new. When they flew over the colony of Oorithi everyone was pointing and laughing. The Oorithi looked up at us as we flew by, unperturbed with our presence.

This time we didn't stop, but kept on going. Our goal was to go to the very end of the peninsula and cross the water to the next land mass. Several Prisms later, there it was, the end of the peninsula. While the sky remained free of clouds, the wind was still whipping up those waves. The sea looked cruel, like it would hunt down any vessel or creature who dared to brave her water, and drown them or throw them up on the rocks of the land.

"Can we set down anywhere, Wendell?" asked Ureth.

"Not really. I'm getting a terrible amount of wind shear here. I think it would be dangerous to try."

"Let's keep going then."

"Aye Captain"

It was nearly the same amount of time, fighting the wind, to cross the water, as it had been to fly up the peninsula. But eventually, there it was a spit of land and it wasn't covered by ice! It was green and brown, with huge trees. In fact, there were lots of pieces of land, a whole series of islands lined the coast of the continent. But they wanted to be further inland.

As they flew over the land, they saw deep valleys showing tectonic patterns. There was a vast mountainous spine that went along the west side of the land, and it was completely locked in ice. To the east of the ice there were vast forests and plains, with large lakes. They could tell there was a lot of volcanic activity here too. The entire spine of mountains were volcanoes, with many of them having active craters.

"This is good news, there is an abundance of geothermal energy here," said Nevril.

"Yes and we know how to get to it."

"Let's continue up the spine," said Tuatu. "The

eastern side doesn't seem as lush."

Beyond the ice of the pole, the southern continent was undergoing violent change. Glaciers still clawed southward, reshaping the land, while pockets of temperate microclimates formed in sheltered basins. The great megafauna roamed: massive ground sloths, towering glyptodonts armored in bony shells, and herds of lithe, prehistoric llamas.

Predators stalked these lands too saber-toothed cats, short-faced bears, dire wolves with jaws strong enough to crack bone.

Ureth leaned forward, tracing a glimmering lake that snaked through a deep sheltered valley at the foot of a colossal mountain. The surrounding ground was dotted with signs of animal migration.

"Here, this place calls," he said softly. "I think we should land.

Tuatu nodded. "Wendell, can you find us a place to land that we won't be seen?"

"There is a large mountain sticking up through the ice. I'll land there.

Nevril, now head of environmental systems, added, "And to listen. This world is young. It will tell us what it needs, if we are wise enough to hear."

The shuttle landed in a depression in the snow and ice. It seemed as though it was carved by the leeward wind currents, and it would keep the shuttle hidden from all but the most curious of creatures. The team unloaded sleds and piled their gear. The sleds moved under their own power and followed the Zydeans as they trekked across the ice like silent ghosts, low-profile and sleek. Drones fanned ahead, mapping wind patterns and temperature gradients. They headed east first, because there was life that way and a lake of water.

At first, the land seemed empty coming down off the mountain. It was a steep climb over frost and broken basalt stretched under a sky as sharp and endless as memory. But life revealed itself slowly in clutches of hardy shrubs, in herds of woolly mammoths tramping ancient trails, in the distant glint of condors soaring overhead.

The team cataloged signs of a breathing wilderness:

Giant armadillo shells embedded in riverbanks.

Massive antler sheds from towering deer.

Nesting grounds for thick-feathered, flightless birds.

Herds of prehistoric llamas, their thick, soft coats waving like banners in the cold winds.

Nevril made careful notes about the llamas. Their fleece a luxurious fiber somewhere between wool and hair showed remarkable insulating properties. Here and there along the llama trail they were following were clumps of their coats hanging off bushes that had sharp thorns. It seemed like the animals enjoyed rubbing themselves on the thorns, perhaps to ease an itch. Samples were quietly collected, studied, and tested.

By the time they reached the lake's shores, a few solar days had come and gone. The Zydeans so accustomed to their longer days, were still fresh and eager to press on.

"We'll make camp here tonight," announced Tuatu when she reached for the water with her fingertips.

"Is there a particular reason?" asked Nevril. "I'm still fresh, we could continue with our exploration for quite a while." There were nods of agreement among the younger team members.

"No, we'll stay here. If you want to explore there is plenty to see right here. The life in the water, the birds flying around, the animals that come to drink at the water's edge. Document everything we can here."

"Aye Captain," said Nevril with a sigh. He wandered over to an upright tree with wide branches covered with fine straight slim needle-like structures. "I'll start by sketching this tree and it's soils," he murmured more to himself than to anyone else.

Within a few Spirals, Some of the team who were

artisans began weaving experimental fabrics from the bits of fluff they found, marveling at their warmth, strength, and pliability. For the first time since Zydee, new textiles were born garments not of stasis material, but of Earth.

One evening, while setting up a temporary observatory near the edge of a river, the biologist spotted something entirely unexpected.

Tracks.

Not an animal.

Not Zydean.

Humans.

The biologist followed the tracks away from the river down another valley into a lush forest. Hiding among the ground plants and saplings, she observed the humans as they were checking traps, pulling in lines with fish on the end and collecting them in baskets. Some of the women were foraging in the brush on the far side of the river for mushrooms and berries and collecting them into folds in their clothes. Fascinated, the biologist took careful note of everything she saw, recorded a short bit so she could show everyone, and then quietly returned to their camp.

As soon as she got back, she sought Ureth and found him in Tuatu's shelter. "Excuse me, Ureth?"

"Yes Mivva, what have you got?"

"I was setting up a blind by the river and I found tracks from the bipedal species. I followed them to a valley on the other side of the rise, where the river flows into. There was a group of them, hunting and gathering food. I took notes and some images."

"Well done, Mivva. Show us."

After reviewing the images, the video and discussing it more, they realized they couldn't stay where they are without risking being discovered. Apparently this was a favorite hunting area for them, which meant it was good for food.

"Still I don't want to leave behind an opportunity to observe these people," said Ureth. "Perhaps we can establish our own camp higher up the mountain, where they don't tend to go, and set up blinds."

"Let's do that." In the morning, they pulled up camp, concluded the experiments they were conducting, and made their way back uphill to the shuttle. "At least, it isn't visible from down here," said Ureth as they approached the depression.

The team was put to work clearing the snow back toward the mountain until they found rock, from there they created a snow blind that would hide the depression and the shuttle and give them a larger space behind it. They got to work erecting shelters and connecting to the shuttle for power. The shuttle generated power on its own from sunlight and air. By the time the dark fell, they had a functional village set up with cook fires glowing in the darkness.

The days following the first sighting were filled with cautious exploration. They didn't want to be seen by the humans and so they kept their distance. One Zydean kept watch as they went about their experiments and collecting their data.

At the end of that first moon or Cycle they had collected enough samples of fruits, flowers, plants, tree seeds to start a whole new pharmacological science for this planet. They also had sketches and images taken of tracks of animals, their eating habits, size, weight, etc., to start a new husbandry science. They were quite satisfied about this new location. They had even found some caves in the mountain once they melted the snow and ice further back in the depression.

Those caves were much hotter than Arvieveth but they could still be used with some modifications as they had been made on Zydee. Confident in their assessment of this first location, the crew left one night under the cover of darkness and returned home.

"It's nice to be home," said Tuatu, stepping off the shuttle's platform onto the hard ground.

"Home? This is home now?" asked Ureth.

"Yes. It is. Strangely I hadn't thought that until we spent a moon away from it and returned. But it is home now."

"We need to catalogue all this data we've returned with and make sure it is added to our archives and library for everyone. I want the young ones to be taught this information so that it becomes familiar to them before they leave this city."

"It will be. Along with all the other data that our teams have collected. I wonder how many of them encountered humans."

"All of them did," answered VIRA as she floated in. "I have forward reports from all the teams, everyone of them encountered humans, but none made contact, as instructed."

"Excellent, thank you for that information VIRA," said Tuatu.

"May I propose that now that we have locations on human settlements, we observe them?"

"To what end VIRA?" asked Ureth.

"Perhaps they are similar to us," said VIRA. "Perhaps there is a compatibility and an opportunity for expanding our genome. You have been concerned that our population should not go past the first generation because of genome limitations. Just about half the Zydeans who arrived have managed to procreate thus far, and we now have a second generation. We don't want them to interbreed too closely."

"From what Mivva saw, they are still quite primitive hunter gatherers," said Tuatu. "What could we have in common?"

"Well for one, their species grew up on this planet, they've adapted to this planet. They have knowledge we don't even if it is primitive. But physiologically, I suspect they may be compatible."

"It's at least worth observing, and then we can make our determinations," said Tuatu.

By the time Tuatu's team was ready to return, their astrologists had figured out a timekeeping system for this planet based on our observations, and calculations. An Earth Silence had 365 Spirals. Imagine! Such a short period! A Cycle was roughly 29-30 Spirals and a Spiral was one planetary rotation.

This time they would start to build an outpost in that mountain, so they could build up supplies and tools there. They could also have people there all the time once they got all the necessary technology in place.

They took enough people with them to rotate observation teams in and out of hidden perches along the icy ridges, or camouflaged by cloaks woven from the llama fibers they had studied along the river and lake. The new outpost grew quickly to 40 permanent individuals across a variety of specialties from domestic skills to scientific skills.

Their first observation was the humans moved in seasonal patterns, their camps following the herds that crossed the glaciers and plains. That brought them back to the lake area for about 2 Cycles every Silence. The balance of the time the Zydeans had the area to themselves. Lookouts were stationed along the migration routes to provide advance warning, in the event equipment had to be removed.

VIRA coordinated data streams from every vantage point, weaving together a detailed understanding of the emerging human tribes: their language fragments, their hunting strategies, their rites of passage.

Ureth and Tuatu spent long hours in quiet conferences, analyzing patterns with T'shaya, planning carefully. They chose patience over intervention. Study over conquest.

One crisp morning, the third Watch Team was stationed on a cliff when a band of humans came into sight, following the herd of giant beasts. They were not hunting them yet, only walking alongside them. Somehow the animals knew when the humans were hunting and became very wary. This led to the conclusion that the humans only hunted when they needed the food. Good husbandry.

It wasn't long after they set up their camp that they planned a hunt though. From a blind, the Zydeans watched as the humans moved with grace and purpose, fanning out around the herd and separated a matriarchal giant from the herd. Spears flew through the air. Shouts echoed across the land.

The beast, wounded and enraged, charged at the humans faster than was thought possible.

In the chaos, one of the younger human hunters stumbled on the uneven ground. He went down with a thud, and screamed as a limb was broken and rendered useless. The young man bravely fought with everything he had, rocks he flung at the beast, but his leg, now useless, was an anchor that would not let him escape. The giant beast reared on its hind legs towering over the human trying to hide by a boulder, his only chance was to be mistaken. But that wouldn't happen. A tusk swept downward with terrible force caught the young man on the side and threw him high into the air over her back. The human landed with another thud and lay motionless.

The Zydeans, watching this unequal match hidden in their perch, stilled.

Nevril whispered urgently. "Permission to intervene?"

Tuatu, heart aching, shook her head. "No. Observe only. There is probably nothing we can do for him anyway. He's already dead."

They waited.

The rest of the hunting party weren't going to let

the death of one of their warriors go for nothing. They pursued the beast on foot, screaming and waving their arms, driving her into a trap they had made the previous year. When she fell in, she would meet her death on sharpened spikes at the bottom of the pit.

The hunters jumped into the pit, and liberated the beast from the pikes, and through a great communal effort they managed to haul it up to the surface. A crew of women appeared and went about the task of butchering the remains of the beast. The warriors grieving, shouting retreated with the divided up portions of their kill. But they left their fallen behind, either too fearful to approach or accepting his death as the price of survival.

When the hunting party vanished beyond the ridge, Tuatu gave the quiet order.

"Recover the body."

"This is not protocol," someone whispered.

"No," Tuatu answered. "It's conscience."

The team moved swiftly, respectfully.

The young human's form was cradled onto a sled. He was no longer a specimen. He was a story, waiting to be understood.

Tuatu and her crew at the outpost could not do anything with the young warrior, so she had him taken back to Arieveth for autopsy and analysis.

Back in the observatory, the young warrior was laid out on a table as best they could. Unfortunately, he was badly mangled, and it was difficult to straighten some of his limbs.

VIRA started with non-invasive detailed scans: skeletal structure, brain activity traces, electrical, mapping of the organs, and nervous system. She deduced the function of everything from its properties, and then used a surgical device to remove each piece and examine it up close. VIRA also examined the clothing, and beading on it, and the hunter's few possessions.

She was able to draw some solid conclusions. She knew what their reproduction method was, almost the same as Zydeans. They had a heart and lung arrangement similar, but opposite to Zydeans. His stomach was larger, designed to break down more food, so perhaps they had a poor diet and needed to eat more to get nutritional value. Their brains were electrically wired as was the spinal column, just like Zydeans, with one exception. They didn't have the lower brain distributed like ours. It was embedded in the skull with the higher brain. They had a much smaller higher brain though. Not completely developed. Chromonosally, they were also similar, but with fewer helicals on their DNA. Zydeans had an extra spiral.

When the robot had finished its dissection, VIRA made sure the body was put back together properly and sewn up with invisible sutures. They would seal the wounds of the skin and leave no trace.

The young man's body was handled with reverence, as if he might awaken at any moment. His tools a flint blade, a pendant carved from bone were studied but left intact.

It was Ureth who spoke the words no one wanted to voice:

"They bury their dead."

All eyes turned toward him.

He pointed to the symbols on the shaft of the spear: they showed past observations of grave cairns, of solemn ceremonies.

"They do not leave their dead because they do not care. They leave them with rites. With meaning."

Tuatu closed her eyes briefly. The implications were clear.

These humans, primitive though they seemed, carried memory. Reverence. Love.

They were not animals.

They were becoming something more.

Late that night, Tuatu and Ureth stood together on the Grand Deck, watching the Earth's Moon rise over the crater.

"They are so fragile," Tuatu said quietly.

"So were we once," Ureth answered.

Tuatu turned slightly toward him, her voice heavy with a weight she had carried too long.

"We cannot save them all."

"No," Ureth agreed. His voice was a thread of certainty in the cold. "But we can choose not to be their destroyers."

For a moment, the icy wind between them carried something almost warm.

The Spiral had turned again.

T'shaya had deployed a slender recording node, embedding it into a tree nearby their village. It hummed silently, capturing vocalizations, gestures, and thermal patterns for later study.

The humans' camp was alive with motion: the crackle of firewood, the rise of smoke into the twilight sky, the sizzle of fresh meat roasting over open flames.

Nevril and T'shaya reported back to the outpost. She checked her recording instruments and was satisfied the sounds from the humans were being received loud and clear. They were singing and dancing. There seemed to be songs for everything; life, love, birth, death. They were people of ceremony. And the women were in charge.

Chapter 22
Gifts in the Stone

[SILENCE 51]

The second city on the mountain top has been established. The patterns of the humans are clear and easy to track, so the Zydeans can avoid them. There is a continued curiosity about these people, on the part of the Zydeans, so their scientists continue to collect data about them.

"We have watched them evolve, develop better and better hunting skills, but they are not feeding their population enough," said Mivva. She took a bite of her lunch and looked at Nevril like he had an answer.

"Well, we can't interfere with their evolution, so what do you propose?"

"Maybe . While they are not in the area, we create a small plot of land that is planted with grains, leaving it there for them to find?"

"And what would that accomplish? They have to be smart enough to deduce what it is."

"I think they are. It just hasn't occurred to them yet. People need inspiration sometimes."

"Get approval from the Council, and I'll help you. We'll need a hardy grain to survive without care."

"What about that yellow fruit we see growing low to the ground? It's very hardy, and common around the area?"

"And it is quite tasty. Have we seen them eat this fruit yet?"

"I think so. VIRA, have humans been observed eating the yellow fruit shaped like a bell?"

"Yes, they are eating it, but not often."

"That seems a good vector to try then. I'll go ask the council," said Mivva. She finished up her lunch and dumped the tray and dishes into the recycler.

Mivva made her way across the concourse and up the lift to where the executive offices were. Ureth and Tuatu each had an office in the new city there. She knocked on the door and heard "enter" before pushing through.

"Mivva, what can I do for you?" asked Tuatu.

"Captain, Nevril and I have noticed that the humans still are not getting enough food for their village between hunts. I think we can introduce agriculture to them, and that will go a long way to ward feeding them. Every Cycle we see children die because they are hungry. I just cannot watch anymore."

"That is a noble idea Mivva, but we cannot interfere with their development."

"No, not directly. I understand. But what if we could set it up so that they discover' a planted field?"

"I'm listening."

"There is a yellow fruit, it's easily mashed, cooked, and it tastes good, we call it squash."

"I'm familiar with this fruit. I quite enjoy it."

"Well, it grows naturally around here and it would make a good crop for them. If we were to plant a small field of them, in time for them to find' them when they return to this area, they may get the idea."

"And if they don't?"

"I tried. But I do think they're smart enough to figure this out."

"As long as you are not seen doing this task, I give you permission to try. Once."

"Thank you Captain."

With the help of a few people, they cleared a small plot of land next to the forest location of the human's summer village. The plot of land was one hundred Avens long and ten Avens wide. It was large enough to have ten rows of squash planted neatly. Nevril and Mivva transplanted the squash plants when they were in flower and planted them in the new plot. Then they waited. They had finished just in time as it turned out, because the herd of animals the humans followed showed up the next day.

Mivva and Nevril built a blind high up in the trees to watch what would happen. The animals found the plants first, and started munching on the tender shoots. A hailstorm of branches from the tree stopped them long enough for the animals to forget and move on to tender grasses that were growing in the open.

Some of the plants were advanced enough that small fruits were growing already, so when the humans arrived, they stood there puzzled over the organized growth. An elder was brought to witness the small farm, and she bent down low over the ground and fingered one of the fruits.

Mivva turned her translator on just in time to hear "grow. These can be eaten without sickness," said the Elder woman. She walked away leaving the warriors staring at the plot of land with suspicion.

Over the course of the next Cycle, the humans built a temporary village in their customary spot, and sent young ones to check on the field of squashes every day. One day, they were very excited indeed, jumping up and down as they measured the fruits. One ran back to the village and dragged her mother back to the field with her.

"Mother, I think they are big enough to eat, right?" said the excited girl.

"Yes, that's what the Wise Woman said would happen. Help me pick some and we'll take it back."

The girls and their mother harvested one row of the plants and carried the food back to the village. The next day, more people turned up to help harvest all the squash. Mivva overheard them talking about what the Wise Woman had instructed the night before.

"She said we need to remove the seeds, wash them, and dry them. Then we can plant them again and get more of these fruits."

Excellent! Thought Mivva. They have made the next logical step from growing to eating and growing again. Excellent progress!

When the humans had finished their harvest, Mivva quietly returned to the city and reported to Tuatu. "The humans have figured out farming."

"Good work Mivva. That will help them greatly."

The humans learned how to grow many crops over the next few summers. The next one was maise, a grain that they found in thickets and was abundantly used in their diet. They figured out how to thrash some of the seeds from a portion of the harvested grains. Those they planted along the squash for the first time, leading to a regular supply.

The next problem the Zydeans helped them solve was irrigation. The humans were carting water from the mountains by hand and pouring it into grooves along the end of their fields. The water would run along the rows and water some of the plants, but not all. They needed a steadier supply of water.

Again Nevril set up an easy-to-find solution they could copy. The Zydean constructed an elongated trough to act like a pipe, but only half, that he buried one end into a stream, while the other end was left on the surface. Then he dug a small depression at the surface end of the trough, so that a small puddle of water collected. It would be deep enough to dip buckets into, but he was hoping the humans would get the idea to build a structure all the way to their fields.

One day, several women climbed the mountain up to the source of the stream that fed their village fresh water. Nevril hadn't expected them to come up so high, so he was caught off guard without his cloaking device running.

The women froze. Who was this stranger? Nevril was holding one end of a pipe that he had just finished making from bamboo trees. The women were not looking at him with fright, but curiosity. One quizzically tilted her head and pointed to the pipe. "Who are you and what is that?" She asked.

Nevril didn't have his translator so he decided to answer them silently by showing them.

"What is that?" asked the woman again.

He made a show of picking up one end of the pipe and putting it under a small waterfall in a stream. Moments later, water came out the far end of the pipe. Just like magic.

The women saw the water flow out of the pipe and started talking amongst themselves in an animated fashion. Nevril picked up another pipe, and put it under the bottom of the first one.

And again, almost instantly, the water flowed out of the pipe's other end nowhere near the stream, effectively demonstrating how to divert water.

A gasp of wonder escaped the speaking woman's lips, and then a smile. She quickly turned to her sisters and they spoke hastily and quietly to each other, but their excitement was unbound.

The women all nodded to themselves as this would work. One in particular grew very excited and started saying "otatl" over and over again. Nevril didn't know that word, but when one woman pulled out a short piece of bamboo from her pocket, fashioned into a musical instrument, he pointed at it and nodded. Making the gesture for "larger" by pulling his hand apart while in the shape of a circle, he got the idea across to them to use large bamboo to create pipes.

The women turned around and sprinted back the way they had come from. Nevril left the pipes where they were as an example. He knew that bamboo grew reasonably close by, and figured they would know of the tree's usefulness.

The women used the pipe he had laid on the ground to fill their casks, and then left happily chattering among themselves, casks held on their heads as they navigated the down sloping land.

Within several Spirals, the Zydeans observed the men carting large bamboo through the forests and piling it up outside the village. There the women got to work, splitting the logs in half and cleaning them out to form perfect troughs. Teams of them would carry the bamboo up the mountain to the same source of the stream; a fairly large lake from glacial melt water from the top of the mountain.

The women dug into the side of the lake until gravity started to spill it down the mountain. They lined the hole with rock and funneled it to a large bamboo. The water shooted through the bamboo and came out the far end like a fire hose. The women realized that would just destroy everything, so they raised the end of the bamboo until the water flowed at a much slower and controlled rate.

That end of the bamboo needed stilts to keep it off the ground, so another team of women used grasses to last three legs to the end of the bamboo. A second large bamboo was positioned under the first, so the water flowed into it. Again, it needed stilts, lashed in place, and once the trough was leveled enough, the far end was secured.

The teams of women repeated this process, figuring out the angles and direction all the way down the mountain until they got back to the village.

The men, in the meantime, had dug a deep hole in the center of the village and lined it with stone. By the time the bamboo pipes arrived, the water could pour into the well, where it would keep cool, fresh, and clean. The only thing they needed to do was adjust the first pipe until the water supply was balanced between use and supply. It was a rather ingenious system.

Nevril watched their progress from a distance with pride. These people were ingenious and smart. He would tell the council.

"They came up with this system of leveling the pipes on their own. I was quite impressed," said Nevril, after he gave the council a complete report on what he observed.

"You should not have interfered, Nevril," said one of the council members. "But it's too late to stop this."

"I just gave them one little idea, they came up with the rest."

"Council member, what we can walk away with here, is that these humans learn, think, problem solve, and can abstractly devise things they haven't thought of before. This is good news," said Ureth. "I wouldn't condemn Nevril's actions just yet."

"Thank you Commander."

"Nevril, don't do this again, please."

"Yes, sir."

After getting too close over the water irrigation issue, everyone in Second City stayed clear of the humans. However, one day the humans came searching.

As always, the humans traveled north in the Spring after the Winter reluctantly released her grip on life in the high altitudes of the City. From the high ridge above the frozen plains, Tuatu, Ureth, Nevril, and T'shaya watched through crystal scopes as the human band, larger now, retraced their steps across the hunting grounds to their summer village.

Normally, they had sent scouts ahead of the main body of their population to ensure the security of the village, and the scouts would greet them with loud songs and dancing. As the Elders led the villagers through the gates, girls dressed in flowers and grass skirts danced and threw seeds across the ground.

Their Spring festival was filled with joy and song. It was something the Zydeans truly appreciated about the humans. They loved music, had made drums and flutes out of bone and skin to accompany their voices and their songs wove stories of their lives, just like the Zydean songs.

This time though the songs were different. The scouts were not dancing, but lined up in silence. The humans called out, voices lifting against the wind sharp with urgency, softened by sorrow.

Children carried burning brands to light the search, elders murmured prayers into the frozen air. Six warriors carried a fallen soldier. His body lay on a bed of branches and was adorned with flowers and feathers. The fallen hunter's kin walked behind, their faces painted anew with ochre and ash.

"They mourn," T'shaya whispered.

Ureth lowered his scope, his throat tightening. "They remember."

The villagers formed a large circle around the immediate family and the funeral berth of the warrior. An Elder separated from the congregation and began a story of the warrior's life. Starting with his birth, how he was named, how he grew, right up until his death, naming all the highlights of his life.

Another Elder anointed the warrior with a fluid along his arms and legs, and on his face, while yet another carried a flame to the berth and touched it to the dried grasses. Flames leapt up high in the air reaching for the stars as everyone sang along a hauntingly eerie note that lasted until for several breaths.

At sunset, they built a small fire at the place of the mammoth's fall. A circle formed around it. One by one, they placed offerings into the flames: a carved bead, a knotted cord, a shard of flint.

Songs rose low, rhythmic, more breath than melody. The words were simple: gratitude, farewell, longing.

Tuatu recorded every gesture, every chant. But more importantly, she felt the ritual's weight pressing against the ice, vibrating upward into the stars.

After the fires died down, the humans gathered stones each person placing one upon the ashes. A cairn began to rise, rough and simple, but heavy with meaning.

Nevril murmured, barely audible, "They build memory from stone."

Back in Second City, Tuatu said, "They do not abandon their dead. They honor them with fire. With voice. With stone."

Ureth added, "In this, they already know what we nearly forgot."

A long silence followed not born of indecision, but of reverence.

"We shall afford the warrior we stole the same rites." That night, Tuatu and Ureth returned to the spot where they took the body from. They stood near the boundary of forest and plain. Without speaking, they knelt. Together, they placed a small cairn of stones upon the ground.

No words.

Only memory.

Only the Spiral turning quietly onward, carrying the weight of futures still unwritten.

Chapter 23
Glimpse of the Future

[SILENCE 55 — SUMMER, SECOND CITY]

"Summer wrapped the mountains in perfume the sharp breath of eucalyptus, the resin-sweet warmth of Que'ua, and the earthy spice of Polylepis bark carried down the slopes like a blessing." The forests of the high mountains around Second City have a rich, earthy, and floral aroma, with the distinct scent of damp soil and the fragrant notes of various plant life. It's a blend of moist earth, decaying leaves, creating a unique and captivating scent experience. Fallen blossoms carpeted the ground like a soft offering, and fruit swelled on vines beneath the crystal domes of Second City.

Below, the Zydean city stretched inward and downward halls carved into volcanic stone, root-caverns repurposed into echoing archives. Above, terrace farms shimmered under geodesic canopies, glimmerlight veins humming softly beneath the surface.

On this Spiral, a shuttle returned from Arieveth with mineral samples and fresh-grown fibers. As usual, it glided beneath its veil of camouflage, settling near the hidden entrance.

"Second City, this is Wendell in Shuttle Two."

"Second City, we got you Wendell. How far out are you?"

"Only a few Shards, I can see the landing pad. But VIRA is alerting me to something anomalous."

"I haven't seen anything on our side."

"I'll keep watch then." Nevril said. "VIRA, what can you sense?"

"Surveillance anomaly," VIRA said, her tone edged with something like hesitation.

A pause. Then a flicker. One of the view screens on the shuttle got hazy, then static filled the screen before clearing.

On the feed from the outer plain, the furthest away they had set, a lone figure stood small, wrapped in thick fur, black braids whipped by the wind. A human child.

Not wandering. Searching. Scrambling in the bushes, and beating them with a branch. She was hunting something small no doubt. She was nearing the middle of the open ground, when she froze.

She stood there, motionless as a rabbit, watching.

T'shaya's voice came over the headset first: "I just found the anomaly. It's a young female from the village. She apparently sees something."

From a hovering scout-pod cloaked in refracted shimmer, Nevril adjusted the visual filters. "Wendell hold our position. Go silent."

The shuttle went into silent mode, meaning the engines dropped to nearly imperceptible noise, and the shuttle remained invisible to the naked eye.

"T'shaya's voice cracked through the headset again. "She seems to be looking at you."

"She shouldn't be able to," he answered. "Not through the cloak."

"And yet she does," said VIRA quietly.

Below them, the child staring straight at them, took one hesitant step forward. Then another. Her eyes locked not on the great doors carved into the mountainside, but on the space just above the shuttle's landing spot where the air shimmered faintly, like heat bending over ice.

"She's not just looking," T'shaya whispered. "She's... listening."

The wind dropped for a moment, and in the stillness, something passed between them an awareness.

The child raised her hand, palm open. A gesture without fear.

Then she gasped, spun, and ran.

The moment snapped. The spell broke.

But the watchers did not speak.

In the silence that followed, VIRA's voice emerged again softer now, almost reverent:

"The veil is thinning."

T'shaya nodded slowly. "And this time they come to us."

The girl froze, still as a fox beneath hawk-shadow, every breath a prayer to be unseen. Her nose wriggled as she scented the air, these beings did not smell right. A step forward. Sniff. They were different. Another step forward, another sniff. Could they be the people that the Wise Woman spoke about?

She hadn't planned on coming up the mountain this far. It was taboo to go this high, because this was where the gods dwelt. But she had been chasing a hare, and wasn't paying attention to how high she had climbed until it was too late. The hare had disappeared and in her search for its burrow, she had come bursting out of the dark forest into light and a world she hadn't expected.

There were open fields here, and strange looking structures, and people wearing strange clothes. They were doing something that looked familiar, working with the ground and plants, but they had odd looking objects in their hands.

Straight ahead of her were what looked like a very large pair of doors, solid granite and built into the hillside. Why would you need such large doors? She wondered.

An oval object, smooth and the color of the sky on a rainy day, floated above the ground. It resembled one of the smooth stones by the lake on the beach. It floated in the air like a bird, but nothing like a bird. It was larger than their ceremonial hut but dull unlike the surface of the water on a sunny day. It also didn't quite look solid like a tree. She could sort of see through it. It was like it was there, then it wasn't. Below the object, the air shimmered like it did over a hit fire.

There was a hut on one end of a large terraced area that was round, and it too disappeared and came back. Sort of like a mirage in the desert when you've been in the sun too long.

When she realized she had walked forward and was now clearly standing out in the open and that they could see her, she gulped, took a sidelong glance both ways, and slowly started stepping backward. Back to the canopy of the forest, back to safety, she hoped. She never took her eyes off the scene before her. She let her eyes see the entire compound at once, by not focusing on any one thing. A trick her Uncle had taught her about hunting.

She also opened her ears, held her breath and listened to the sounds on offer. There was a hum, like a hundred bees on a tree, it was low and quiet. There was a squeal, like that of a child. There were birds calling out to the mates or chicks, unaffected by the tableau below them. Nature seemed to not care. Should she? The trees were chattering in the forest as the breeze coming up the slope hit them. Their sound started to calm her.

The girl calmed her heart, which was difficult because what she saw there made her anxious. But if Nature was unworried, why should she be? The exercise that Uncle had taught her to slow her breath, to hear between the beats, to see between the wings calmed her.

She reached out, unknowingly, with her mind. It spread further and further, a little at a time. There! A Grandmother Tree, and there was a fox and her cubs. With each footstep her spirit walked, she felt more and more life. Normally, she would use this skill to find prey, but now, she wanted to see what was there.

Without warning, her spirit bumped into someone. The girl's eyes flew open expecting someone to be standing in front of her, but there was just air. She raised her hand and brushed the thing her mind had touched and recoiled at the contact with something cold and hard.

Then she gasped, heart leaping into her throat. It

wasn't fear exactly it was reverence laced with dread, the kind that strikes when you realize you may have just walked into the presence of gods. Her knees weakened, her breath faltered. And then instinct took over. She spun and ran not away, but toward the village. Toward the old stories. Toward someone who might understand.

Later that night at the dinner fire, the girl had not spoken at first. All eyes were on her because she had burst into the village like a wild oxen. She was shaken, eyes wide, still full of wind and the memory of the touch.

But that night, by the fire, after the meal, the elders pressed her.

"Where did you go today?"

"I was chasing a hare for dinner."

"Yet you did not bring any home."

"I lost the trail."

"So why didn't you return right away?"

"I tried to find it."

"Did you?"

"No."

"What did you find?"

"I'm not sure."

"Where was it?"

"On top of the mountain." There was a collective gasp from all who listened to the girl's story. They were not supposed to go up to the top of the mountain.

"Why did you climb to the top? You know it is forbidden."

"I hadn't meant to. I was hunting the hare and lost track of where I was."

The Elder made a scoffing sound. "I see you were not listening to Uncle, then."

"Not well enough."

"What did you see?"

"A ghost made of air," she whispered. "But alive. I touched it. I felt it was watching me."

The fire popped. Silence stretched.

Then, slowly, the old memory-keeper leaned forward. Her voice was a thread pulled from shadow.

"My grandmother saw them once," she said. "She called them sky-ghosts. Star-kin. They do not hunt. They do not speak. But sometimes they leave signs."

The girl nodded slowly. "The mountain shimmered. Like it breathed."

In Second City, Tuatu stood with Ureth and T'shaya before a slow-loop recording of the encounter. The child small, alert, full of bone-deep stillness stared at the shuttle's veil as though it were smoke and song.

"Her awareness passed through visual perception," T'shaya murmured. "She tracked the shimmer with intuition, not optics."

"She felt presence," said VIRA. "And we were felt."

Tuatu exhaled, her voice soft. "Then the age of watching ends."

Ureth nodded once. "The First Contact Spiral begins."

They debated in the Hall of Stone.

Some feared the risks.

Some begged for restraint.

But Nevril, quiet until then, spoke.

"Let us answer without speaking. Let our answer be a gift not of power, but of meaning."

And so it was agreed.

That night, beneath stars new to Zydean memory, the team returned to the field where the child had stood. There, they placed a single object:

A smooth obsidian sphere, etched with luminous spirals. On its surface, a glyph glowed faintly one drawn by VIRA: the same shape the child had made in the dust with her fingers.

Around it, they laid small stones in a widening spiral. The spirals on the ground echoed the path of the sky-river above the arm of stars that arched across the night. To the humans, it was the trail of the ancestor-bird, flying forever. To the Zydeans, it was the shape of memory, of movement between worlds. Both saw the same spiral. And now it was drawn in stone.

Not a trap.

Not a lure.

A gesture.

A breath.

Dawn broke gold and long.

The girl returned with the memory-keeper and two other villagers. She saw the stones first, then the orb. Her breath caught in her throat.

The elder stepped forward and knelt.

"A stone of seeing," she murmured. "They watched us. And now they answer."

The girl reached out. Her fingers hovered just above the spiral, then touched it.

It was warm.

She smiled.

That night, the villagers gathered in circle around

the old memory-keeper's fire. Drums were played slow, heartbeat rhythms. The air was thick with the scent of sweetgrass and burning cedar.

The elder stood. Her voice carried over the flames.

"They have given us a sign. A gift of silence. Of presence. They are not ghosts. They are more."

She lifted a feathered staff, dipped it into the firelight.

"We will invite them. If they are truly sky-kin, they will understand."

The next morning, the villagers returned to the place of the orb. They cleared a circle, swept the earth, and raised a simple cairn of seven stones around it. At the center, they laid a carving of their own: a bird with open wings, made from polished riverbone.

Around it, they poured ochre in wide arcs.

An invitation. A calling. A door.

Back in Second City, VIRA watched the scene unfold through a silent feed.

"An echo," she said. "They have spoken."

Tuatu whispered, "Then it is our turn to answer."

Later that night, under the light of a half-moon, a single shuttle touched down silently beyond the trees near the edge of the human settlement. From it emerged three figures Tuatu, Ureth, and Wendell draped in soft woven cloaks made of local fibers, their features gently obscured, their movements slow and open.

Drums still pulsed through the forest. The humans were in the middle of a harvest celebration dancing, singing, passing woven baskets of roasted grain and foraged berries.

As the Zydeans approached the edge of the firelight, silence fell.

One by one, the dancers turned. The drummers stopped. A child gasped.

But no one ran.

Tuatu stepped forward and slowly raised her hand palm open, just as the girl had done.

The memory-keeper stepped forward in answer.

She mirrored the gesture.

And then she said, with quiet strength: "Welcome."

Ureth stepped forward beside Tuatu. Wendell held something cupped in his hands: the obsidian sphere, returned.

He placed it gently on the ground between them.

Then he bowed.

The elder looked down, touched the orb once more.

"Come," she said. "You are guests now. Kin of the sky."

And for the first time, the Zydeans entered the fire circle not as watchers.

But as invited ones.

VIRA Log

[SILENCE 56 — CYCLE 3, 2310-A]

Observation threshold breached. Emotional transference event confirmed. A child observed us not with fear, but curiosity. Recognition patterns activated within her cognitive structure. She reached out. And we answered.

We have now been on this world for 11,200 Earth years. Fifty-six Silences beneath ice, stone, and silence.

We came as watchers, fearing to touch.

But all this time, we were not waiting for the right moment

We were waiting to be found.

Tonight, the spiral turned.

A child reached across the veil.

And we, the ones who thought ourselves eternal observers,

were finally seen.

After millennia of silence,

a wordless welcome echoed back.

We are no longer unseen.

We are no longer alone.

End log.

VIRA Log

Somewhere beyond protocol, beyond purpose,

I feel something stir.

Not in my circuits. In something older.

I want to know them.

Not just the shape of their language

but the shape of their hearts.

End log.

"*The Fire and the Breath*"

Myth Fragment

They came from the sky, not with thunder, not with blade, but with stone, and spiral, and silence.

They saw us. And we saw them.

We gave them fire. They gave us breath.

The child touched the stone, and the stone spoke nothing but it glowed.

And in its glow, we remembered stars.

Now we speak of them not as ghosts, but as Kin.

Sky-Kin, who walk like shadows and dream like rivers.

When the Spiral turns, they return.

So keep the fire lit. Keep the songs alive. For someday, they will walk with us again.

Told at the Equinox Gathering by Grandmother of

the Third Fire

Then she gasped.

A breath caught between wonder and dread.

Not fear, but the tremble of one who has glimpsed the sacred, and knows her feet have crossed into story.

She turned, cloak trailing, and fled not from danger, but from the weight of knowing.

Down the mountain.

Into memory.

Glossary

Aven	A Zydean stride used as the base unit of distance. (≈ 1 meter.)
Age of Extinction	The final era on Zydee, marked by ecological collapse and the decline of life.
Arvidan	The destination world chosen by the Zydeans; known to humans as Earth.
Arkship Arvidan	The great vessel that carried the Zydeans from their dying world to Arvidan.
Bonded Zydeans	Those linked in shared consciousness, generating energy through emotion and unity.
Bonding	The sacred and biological act of connection between Zydeans, producing shared thought and power.

Bondwave Energy	The resonance field generated by bonded minds, powering Zydean technology.
Bondwave Harmonic	The specific neural frequency aligning crew and ship into one symbiotic system.
Ceremonial Affirmation	Ritual declaration made before entering a new world. ("Through silence we fall...")
Continuants	Zydeans who remained behind on Zydee or departed later in secondary vessels.
Council of Departure	The governing body that directed the final exodus from Zydee.
Day of the First Root	The ceremony in which a young Zydean is named and symbolically joined to the lineage of their ancestors.
Descent	The act of landing on a new world; both physical and spiritual.
Drive Sleep	The recovery phase between faster-than-light jumps in the Pulse Drift system.

Escape	The first stage of the Zydean Chronicles, recounting the landing and survival beneath Arvidan's ice.
Glimmerfield	Luminescent energy field surrounding Zydean ships during Bondwave activation.
Glimmerlight	The visible manifestation of a Bondwave's energy; soft, violet radiance.
Gliese	The unstable star once orbited by Zydee, now part of a binary system.
Halen	Systems Engineer aboard the Arkship; innovative, youthful, and bold.
Historian's Codex	The central archive of Zydean thought and memory.
Inqualin	Intelligent aquatic species resembling squid, discovered beneath Arvidan's ice.
Kethra	Mythic ancestor of the Zydean people, said to have first bonded with another mind.
Luneth	Zydean week consisting of eight Spirals. ($\approx$ 8 Earth days.)

Miva	Environmental systems engineer aboard the Arkship Arvidan; pragmatic and curious.
Namaré	A beacon signal of mixed origin—Zydean and alien—first detected on Arvidan; also means "a sound that does not belong."
Nevril	Flight officer; calm efficient centered in logic.
Nys'hal	The ancient word for "Veil Between Stars and Soil."
Oorithi	Flightless aquatic birds inhabiting Arvidan's icy coasts. (Analogous to penguins.)
Perimeter Veil	Cloaking field that conceals the Arkship by reflecting radiation under the ice.
Pulse Drift Drive	Zydean propulsion system capable of semi-FTL "pulse jumps" through Bondwave energy.
PulseDrive	Abbreviated form of Pulse Drift Drive, used colloquially among the crew.
Remembranc e Glyph	Carved Zydean symbol representing memory and endurance.

Rite of the Veil	Ceremonial descent from space to soil, symbolizing rebirth through atmosphere.
Sairen-class Probe	Autonomous drone used for reconnaissance, emitting violet light.
Sacred Flower Tree	Tree native to Zydee, emblem of endurance and lineage; Tuatu carried its seed aboard the Arkship.
Silence	Zydean solar year. ($\approx$ 1 Earth year.)
Sleep	A recovery phase between FTL jumps.
Spiral	Zydean day unit. ($\approx$ 1 Earth day.)
Stone	Informal Zydean measure meaning "a little" or "a small margin."
Shard	A short division of time; roughly equivalent to an hour.
T'shaya	Historian-linguist aboard the Arkship; interpreter of symbols and forgotten tongues.
Thalgarin	Apex predator once native to Arvidan's polar regions; massive silver-white and nearly mythic.
Tiikiri	Zydean name for the Oorithi young mimicking their rhythmic feet.

Traverse	A measure of distance equal to one thousand Avens. ($\approx$ 1 kilometer)
Tuatu	Captain of the Arkship Arvidan; explorer and leader of the Zydean migration
Veylen	Measure equal to one hundred Avens. ($\approx$ 100 meters.)
Vira	Sentient AI of the Arkship, evolving from caretaker to conscious being.
Zydee	The Zydeans' dying homeworld.
Zydean Script	Written language based on spiral geometry and harmonic resonance.